THE AUTOBIOGRAPHY OF AN INDIAN PRINCESS

Sunity Devee,
Maharani of Cooch Behar

Originally Published 1921

TABLE OF CONTENTS

Chapter I

MY CHILDHOOD

I was born in 1864 at the old house known as "Sen's House" which my great-grandfather built at Coolootola, a part of Calcutta where many of our family lived. My birth was always remembered in connection with a storm which occurred when I was six days old, a most important time to a Hindu baby, for then the Creator is supposed to visit the home, and write upon its forehead the little one's fate. Perhaps people will think the stormy weather in the beginning signified a stormy future for me.

No girl could have been more fortunate in her parents than I. My father, the great Keshub Chunder Sen, is considered one of the most remarkable men India has ever produced, and my dear mother belonged to the best type of Hindu woman. Gentle, loving, and self-denying, her whole life was beautiful in its goodness and its simplicity.

The story of a great religious movement is not one which can be told at length in a book of memories. The religion for which my father suffered and which will be for ever connected with his name is the Brahmo or Religion of the New Dispensation, a religion of tolerance and charity. To quote my father's words, "The New Dispensation in India neither shuts out God's light from the rest of the world, nor does it run counter to any of those marvellous dispensations of His mercy which were made manifest in ancient times. It simply shows a new interpretation of His eternal goodness, an Indian version and application of His universal love."

My readers do not perhaps quite know the meaning of Brahmo. A Brahmo is a person who believes in Brahmoe (One God). There is a Hindu god called Brahmuna, with four heads—Brahmoe is not that god. Some Western people may think Brahmins are the same as Brahmos. Once I remember an English lady saying to me: "I met some Brahmo ladies...." I asked, "How did you know they were Brahmos?" "Because they wore lace on their heads." Others have an idea that all advanced Indian ladies must be Brahmos.

If my readers by some good fortune have read ancient Indian history they will know what the real Indian religion was. There was one God and no belief in caste, in fact there was no such thing as caste. Caste meant a different thing in those days. It referred to character and life. A Brahmin lived a pure and holy life, and preached religion. Next to the Brahmins were the Katnyas; they were rulers, fighting people; they guarded their families, states, and countries. Then came the Sudhras, who served the others. But now there are hundreds of different castes, which makes people rather narrow-minded, for if one believes in caste one can never believe in universal brotherhood.

From the days of his youth my father was earnest and devout. He must have gone through much trouble of mind before he decided to fly in the face of family tradition and take a step which meant partial separation from his nearest and dearest. My mother was a member of a strict Hindu family, and their marriage had been solemnised with Hindu rites; but she did not fail him in the hour of trial. I have often heard my mother talk of the difficulties of those days, before she left Coolootola with my father. When he announced his approaching conversion, the "Sen House" was plunged into a state of agitation, and my mother was by turns entreated and threatened by angry and dismayed relatives. "Do not go against our customs," urged the purdah ladies. "You are one of us. Your place is here. You must not renounce your caste. Imagine the results of such a dreadful sin." When thus reproached, the young girl dreaded the horrors of the unknown. It may be that she wavered; but if so, it was not for long; and it was arranged that she should go with my father to be converted by the Maharshi D. Tagore. On the day fixed for their departure a note came. My father had written simply, "I am waiting." Then my mother knew she must decide her future for good and all. All the relations were screaming, crying, and threatening my mother, saying that she would bring disgrace on the family by leaving the house, and thus losing her caste. But it did not hinder her, because of those three simple words—"I am waiting"—the call of Love. When she realised their meaning, she threw off the fetters of the past and went forth to meet her destiny. There was a round staircase used by the purdah ladies where she knew my father awaited her. The trembling girl hurriedly traversed corridors and verandahs until she reached it. Fearfully she descended the dark steps, her heart beating with fright, until at last she saw my father. He said quietly: "I want you to realise your position fully. If you come with me, you give up caste, rank, money, and jewels. The relations who love you will become estranged from you. The bread of bitterness will be your portion. You will lose all except me. Am I worth the sacrifice?"

My mother had had a most beautiful and wonderful vision, which is too sacred for me to relate. This gave her strength and courage, she did not hesitate but descended the steps and joined my father. It was a moment too wonderful for words. They looked into each other's eyes. He read perfect faith and courage in hers. She saw in his a love which gave her confidence to face the future. They passed down the corridor and found themselves in the first courtyard opposite the great entrance, where the durwans (gatekeepers) were standing on guard.

Twice my father ordered the durwans to open the door, but they did not move. It was very still in the courtyard. My mother was frightened. This was a strange adventure, and hitherto she had hardly seen a man except her husband. A trembling, slim girl, she stood near my father with her head-dress pulled quite low. Across the door there was a huge iron bar, which was too heavy for one man to lift. My father, seeing that the durwans would not open the door, went to lift the bar and did so quite easily. Then a voice was heard speaking from the upper floor. It was my father's eldest brother. He had watched all that had happened, and, seeing that my parents were determined, he decided to let them go. "Let them pass, and open the gate," he called out to the durwans. The wondering durwans threw open the door, and my parents passed from the shadows into the sunlight.

My father took my mother to the beautiful house of Maharshi Debendra Nath Tagore. The household were all waiting to welcome them, though they had great doubts whether my father would be able to bring my mother away from such a strict Hindu family. The Maharshi introduced my mother to his daughters as if she had been his own child. Although a rich man's daughter-in-law and a rich youth's wife, my mother was wearing a simple sari with hardly any jewels. She always spoke of the great kindness and affection she received from this family, and she deeply revered the old Maharshi. We have always felt that there is a great bond between our two families.

My parents remained away for some time during which my father's formal conversion took place. After some months my grandmother and uncle begged him to return, and gave him a small house near the big house. There my parents lived until my father fell seriously ill, and his eldest brother declared that, in spite of all difficulties, he must come back to the old home. He came back, and after long suffering and much careful nursing grew well again. My dear old grandmother and all my aunts and uncles were very glad to have my father and mother back among them. A few months later my eldest brother was born, and the Maharshi Debendra Nath Tagore gave him the name Karuna.

The new arrangement was not without its trials. Our branch of the family had lost caste, and we underwent all kinds of vexations in consequence. One great trouble was with the servants. No Hindu would wait upon us, and a procession of cooks who objected to "Christians" (any one who was not a Hindu in those days was called a Christian) came and went. My father's happy nature enabled him, however, to rise above such discomforts, and, as he was cheerfully seconded by my mother, caste soon had no terrors for us.

Our days were full of interest, and some of my earliest recollections are connected with the female education movement which my father started. There was an establishment called the Asram where his followers from all different classes lived in happy disregard of caste and class. This house was quite close to

Coolootola, and there I spent many happy days with my sister-in-law, then Miss Kastogir, the ideal of my girlhood.

I remember another delightful house which a friend lent to my father for his people. It was a beautiful place with two big buildings in its grounds. In these houses the Asram people came and lived for months, and we stayed there too. I have the happiest memories of this Belghuria garden-house; it always seemed to me a Paradise on earth. I was a little girl when I first went there, but I never smell a rose without recalling the vanished perfume of the roses in that wonderful garden. There were roses everywhere. They scattered my path with scented softness, and turned their flushed or sweetly pale faces to meet my wondering eyes. Roses of youth … the fairest. Are any others ever so treasured?

We were not allowed to pluck the fruit or flowers in the Belghuria garden, and I remember seeing cards in my father's clear handwriting fixed on the trees, which forbade us to hurt the growing loveliness.

My father had indeed a striking personality: tall and broad-shouldered, he gave one the impression of great strength. I always thought of him as an immortal; his eyes were "homes of silent prayer." Lord Dufferin once remarked to me: "I did not know you were Mr. Sen's daughter. I've travelled far and seen many handsome men, but never one so handsome." Sir A. A. Chowdhuri's father once said: "Mr. Keshub is no ordinary man, as you can tell by the perfect shape of his feet and the pink sole." And my dear husband often said, "A sculptor would give anything to have your father's foot as a model." The expression of his face, people said, was like that of Buddha, calm and quiet. His voice was gentle, yet clear, and even by a large crowd every word could be distinctly heard. He had wavy hair and wonderfully white even teeth, and there was always a smile on his face. My father was quite indifferent to caste, although the Brahmo creed as first practised by Maharshi Debendra Nath Tagore and his followers included it, and this caused a split between my father and his old friend. They disagreed on this point, and finally my father left the Maharshi Tagore, first because of the question of caste, and secondly, because of the Maharshi's jealousy of my father's influence with his followers. I remember hearing people talk of the powerful influence of my father's teachings. Even men with large families gave up their occupations to follow him. They looked upon him as almost a divinity, and I myself believe he was gifted with extraordinary powers, as the following strange incident seems to prove.

In a house at Monghyr, a few hours' journey from Calcutta, my father lived at one time with his followers. One morning, after the usual service was over, a gentleman who had been present waited hoping my father would say he need not go to the office that day. As my father, however, said nothing he left looking very sad. After some time my father said to his followers: "You did not want Mr. to go?"

"No, we hoped you would let him stay," was the reply.

"Do you want him to come back?"

"Well, he's about a mile away; how can any one overtake him?"

My father smiled and asked for a khole (a sort of drum), and struck it gently, calling the gentleman by name as he did so. It seems incredible, but is nevertheless true, that the person thus summoned heard the call as he stood under a tree by the roadside. "I hear him," he cried, "I am to return," and to the great surprise of all he did return, and related how he had heard his name called.

My father used to tell us stories from the Bible and other sacred books, and I remember how much impressed we were with the story of the Ten Virgins. He described it so well that we could see the whole thing, and I remarked: "We must be careful not to run out of oil or to fall asleep when the bridegroom is coming." He also told us many other stories, and one was a particular favourite.

There was once a rich Maharajah who was very fond of mottoes and sayings, and always rewarded handsomely any person who brought him a new one.

In a village near his palace lived four Brahmin brothers who were so poor they often could not get their daily meal. One day they said to each other: "Our Maharajah is generous, he richly rewards those who bring him words of wisdom. Let us try and make some." These Brahmin brothers were not only poor but stupid, and could think of nothing. Although by the next day they were not ready for the visit, they made up their minds to go and see what they could do. On the way the eldest brother suddenly stopped saying: "I have got it, I have got it. I am sure I shall receive a handsome present." The other three were very much excited and eagerly asked what it was. "I saw a rat," he said, "and I thought: 'Silently he picks a hole in the wall.'" The brothers thought this splendid and looked forward to a great reward. A little further on the second brother stopped, saying: "I have got one too." "What is it?" they asked. "Bump, bump, bump, he jumps." "How did you think of it?" they asked. "Did you not see a frog jumping from one side of the road to the other?" After a while the third brother shouted: "Mine is the best." "What is yours?" they asked excitedly. "Hither and thither he looks." "What does that mean?" they inquired. "Did you not see a squirrel on the branch looking here, there, and everywhere?" When the palace came in sight the youngest brother was in tears; he could think of nothing. "You will all receive your presents," he said, "I must wait without for you." But when they arrived at the door and the kobal took their message to the Maharajah the youngest brother's face beamed and he followed the others into the ruler's presence.

Each had written his saying upon a piece of paper and it was placed upon a tray. After a while the Maharajah said, "It grows late. Return for your rewards to-morrow, when I shall have read your papers," and the brothers, bowing, retired. Towards midnight the Maharajah awoke and bethought himself of the papers brought by the four poor brothers, and of his promise to read them. He rose from his bed and went towards the window, that looked out upon the terrace of the palace, with the papers in his hand. Now it chanced that just at that moment the kobal (page-boy) was under the window trying to make a hole through the wall through which to enter and murder the Maharajah. Suddenly he heard the voice of the Maharajah. "Silently he picks a hole in the wall." Terrified the kobal left the hole and hopped across the terrace. "Bump, bump, bump, he jumps," the Maharajah continued. The kobal stopped, looking this way and that in his panic. "Hither and thither he looks," the voice went on. The trembling kobal tiptoed away, but the voice reading the youngest brother's paper followed him: "The kobal walks on the marble, thud, thud, thud." Convinced now that the Maharajah could see him and knew everything, the wretched kobal fled. Next morning he went to one of the officers of the palace, and falling at his feet confessed his intended crime and told how the Maharajah had seen all he did. The officer at once went to the Maharajah and told him the whole story. When the four poor brothers arrived soon after at the palace they were amazed to receive as a reward for their sayings, thousands and thousands of rupees, while the youngest was given a house and provision for life, the Maharajah saying he would ever be grateful to him for having saved his life.

Coolootola was the starting point for many of our religious excursions. We always delighted in these journeys, as they meant "seeing things." One of the missionaries, Kaka Babu, who had charge of the money and arranged all the details of our everyday life, took care of my eldest brother and me. We travelled sometimes by train, and sometimes in a box-like horse carriage, which was rather uncomfortable, yet I have gone from Agra to Jaipur in it.

A certain visit we made to Etawah interested us very much. The house intended for our use was not ready, and we were obliged to spend the night in an old place which had once been a public building. My mother could not sleep, for she had a feeling of horror although there seemed at first nothing to alarm her. But before long she beheld a most awful vision, which lasted the rest of the night. She saw in the huge hall soldiers in red uniforms and Indians struggling together; great pools of blood were on the floor, and women and children were weeping. At first my mother thought it was only a dream; but when she opened her eyes she saw it as vividly as when they were closed, and terrified she longed for the dawn. At daybreak she told my father of the vision. He was surprised, as were his followers; for years before during the Mutiny a massacre had actually taken place in the hall. My father had not told my mother lest she should be nervous; when she heard the story my mother insisted on moving into another house, and we left then and there.

I remember a journey to Jubbalpore when I first realised the devotion of Indian wives to their husbands. We drove to a little house built upon a rock among the hills, about which there was this story:

"In bygone times a certain Maharajah was going to fight the Mohammedans, and his wife, who loved him, wished to accompany him.

"It is impossible," he said. "How can you go with me?" "I will not remain alone in the palace," she answered firmly. "But I am going to fight." "No matter, my place is by your side." "You cannot come with me."

The loving Maharani then said to her husband: "I came to this palace as your wife, your Maharani. I shall not remain in the palace without you, my lord, my husband, my Maharajah, not even for an hour. If I am not allowed to go to the battlefield with you, I, your Maharani, will leave the palace and go wherever you like to send me. If it is your fate to return victorious, I shall return as your Maharani to the palace."

The husband, although a commander and a ruler, spoke to her very gently in a voice full of love and sympathy: "My beautiful little wife, where will you go? How can I leave you in discomfort? You are my Maharani and do not know the hardships of the world."

"Oh," she said, "my lord, do you think that I would be happy without you in this place of luxury and wealth? No, my lord, let me go. You and I will leave the palace together. You are going to fight for your country, my brave and handsome young husband, and I, your little wife, will be thinking of you and your love wherever I may be."

The story goes that the Maharajah granted his wife's request, and had this little house built in one night on a single piece of rock among the hills. There she anxiously awaited news of him. Alas! the enemy was victorious and the Maharajah killed. Never would he return and take her from that place of waiting, back to the palace where they had lived and loved.

Then came the supreme act of devotion, the willing sacrifice. The widowed Maharani offered herself, to the flames upon a funeral pyre near the house on the rock, and I remember that, as darkness fell in that lonely spot, I felt as if I were living in another world. My childish heart vaguely wondered what that love could be which made people careless of life. The future was then mercifully as obscure as the evening shadows. I was to know later that the agony of the fire is nothing compared with the fierce flames of aching remembrance. The pang of death is happiness compared with the weary time of waiting to rejoin the beloved husband who has gone before. The little house is still standing.

The childhood of an Indian girl of years ago may have some interest now, and I must say that I do not admire the modern upbringing of children. Our old system had many defects, but it had also many advantages, chiefly the ideas of simplicity and duty which were primarily inculcated in the little ones. Religion was never uninteresting to us and lessons were a pleasure. I was the second of ten children, and named after Sunity, the mother of Dhruba. I got up early and by nine o'clock my eldest brother, "Dada," and I were ready for school. I went to Bethune College and he to a boys' school. We came back at four. I had a second bath. My hair was arranged and I had a meal of fruit and sweets. Then came the glorious hour of fun and freedom when the innumerable children of "Sen's House" played together.

My mother always helped Dada and me prepare our lessons in both English and Bengali, and we always prayed with her in a small room next to our bedroom. There we were taught little mottoes: "Always speak the truth," "Respect and obey your parents." Once I had a very high fever and my mother told me not to go to school, but I loved my school, and when my mother had gone to the service I had my bath quietly and dressed, and went off in the school bus. After a short time I shivered so much that Miss Hemming, one of the teachers of whom I was very fond, put me on a couch, covered me up well, and when I felt a little better sent me home. How often I felt and still feel that I suffered because I disobeyed my dear mother.

Looking back on those days of childhood I have vivid memories of their happiness. The great house seemed an enchanted palace. It is difficult to convey to English readers a real idea of the fascination of its cool, silent interior with the six courtyards, and the deep wells which supplied drinking and bathing water. In the zenana part of the establishment where the strict purdah ladies lived, the rooms ran round one of these courtyards, and the ladies were never allowed to walk outside it. When they went into town, the "palkis" came right inside to fetch them. I remember wonderful games of hide-and-seek which we children played about the courtyards and the old house. I was too young then to understand what "conscience' sake" meant.

The whole of the domestic arrangements at Coolootola were on patriarchal lines, and strange to relate, family quarrels were rare, although there was a very large number of women living together under the same roof. When I say that our household included fifty relations, some idea of the size of the establishment will be arrived at.

As I grew older I began to feel that I was rather an outsider in the festivities which the other girls enjoyed, and I discovered this was due to my loss of caste, but, as every one at Coolootola was very fond of me, I soon threw aside my real or imaginary troubles. I used to ran about the zenana, and admire my pretty cousins, who seemed to pass their time doing woolwork slippers for their husbands. They never liked people to know this, and the wools and canvas were hurriedly hidden when any one came in. The mothers looked after the housekeeping and played cards in their leisure time. I remember one aunt who was famous for her card parties.

My grandmother, who was very handsome, was the head of the house. She exacted and received the utmost deference from her daughters-in-law, who never dared to speak to their husbands in her presence. She had a warm corner in her heart for me. I was never afraid of her, although I used to wonder whether I should be like the other ladies when I grew up.

My grandmother Thakoorma was a grand cook. Although she was a rich man's daughter-in-law, my grandmother cooked and did the household work as if she were in a poor house. She and her sister-in-law used at one time to hide their brooms under their beds, each meaning to try and get up earlier than the other to clean the room; such was their delight in their housework.

The afternoon was the most delightful time of the day, for then we bathed, dressed our hair, and arrayed ourselves in dainty muslin saris preparatory to going on the roof. I loved that hour, and the memory of it often comes back to me. I close my eyes and dream I am a child again sitting in the midst of that happy group, and can almost feel the welcome breeze once more fanning my face. As we sat and told stories we sometimes caught glimpses of a splash of colour on the roof of distant houses and knew that other girls were also enjoying the cool of the day.

I used always to associate perfume and soap with my married cousins; in fact, I believed that some people married on purpose to get unlimited supplies of soap and scent. "You won't get married, Sunity," the cousins would laugh. "Oh yes, I will," I would reply. "Then I shall have lovely perfumes, and as much soap as I want."

The young wives were never allowed to see their husbands during the day; but often when I played in the front courtyard I heard my name called softly and would be asked to convey love-letters between the temporarily separated couples, who found time long without each other in the first days of wedlock.

I also remember the open air operas (jatras) which were performed in the field close to the house. The advent of the players was always the signal for my father's youngest brother to nail down the shutters on that side of the house if he thought the acting of the jatras not quite proper for the ladies to hear.

One of our customs is for young girls to make vows as they worship before symbolic figures made of flour, or painted on the ground. "May I have a good husband," prays one. "May I be rich," sighs her worldly-minded sister. Marriage and wealth are as important in the East as in Mayfair. My vows, ordered by my father, were planned on different lines, and usually excited pity or amusement. I promised to give money to the poor, never to tell a lie, to feed animals and birds, and to give people cool beverages during the hot weather.

Oh happy days: I can still smell the incense which burnt before the idol at twilight when the elder ladies made their devotions. From across the gulf of time I can hear the faint tinkle of the bells, and the peace of the past pervades my soul. It was a heavenly feeling when Arati (evening prayer) time came and the elderly ladies, among whom the most prominent figure was that of my dear old grandmother, bowed themselves in homage to their god in the sanctuary. The conch shells and the bells sounded, the flowers and the incense gave out their delicious perfume, and family life seemed to me heavenly and pure.

Chapter II

MY FAMILY

The Asram near Coolootola consisted of two houses joined together, and there we lived for a time with many of my father's followers as one big united family (a thing hitherto unheard of in India), addressing each other as sisters and aunts, uncles and brothers. My father held a service in the hall every morning. His motto was "Faith, Love, and Purity," and upon this he always acted. His life was a pilgrimage of extraordinary faith which made him trust in the infinite mercy of God even in the darkest hour, of love which enabled him to view the failings of others with perfect charity and compassion, and purity which kept the lustre of his private life undimmed to the last.

My father formed a Normal School for our girls, called the Native Ladies' Normal School. This school was at one time the only institution of the kind in India. To-day there are hundreds of colleges and schools all over India for Indian girls and women. My father fought for female education. How keenly he was opposed by the leading men at the time! Curiously enough, some of the men who spoke most strongly against female education were the first to bring their wives out of purdah; indeed, to my idea, they are now too English. Later on my father established a college in Calcutta named after her late Majesty Queen Victoria. This college will always be associated with the name of Keshub Chunder Sen. He did not believe in the importance of university degrees; he maintained that for a woman to be a good wife and a good mother is far better than to be able to write M.A. or B.A. after her name. Therefore, only things likely to be useful to them were taught to the girls who attended the Victoria College. Zenana ladies also came to the lectures, and the good work flourished. I always remember the name of Miss Pigot in connection with the educational movement in India. She was the head of an institution close to where we lived. One of the objects of this institution was to train Christian Indian girls to visit Hindu houses and give lessons to the women who wished to improve their education. Miss Pigot also took charge of Hindu ladies while their husbands were in England. She always showed the greatest interest in our family, and called my grandmother "Mother."

Miss Pigot is still alive; I am very fond of the dear old lady, she has been a true friend to us all.

Sadhankanan was the name of the country house belonging to my father, not far from Calcutta, in which we lived later on. The house itself was small, but the grounds were charming with their beautiful trees, flowers, and fruit. There we lived an open-air life among the flowers by which the air seemed always perfumed. I remember a curious thing happening there which filled me with fresh admiration for my father and helped to make me think he was more than human. The gardens at Sadhankanan were full of snakes. As I stood by a hedge of pineapple trees one day, I suddenly saw a frog hopping at a tremendous pace in the direction of the praying-ground where my father and his followers were engaged in their devotions; it was chased by a snake. The frog jumped straight on to my father's knees, and the pursuer, stopping bewildered in front of his quarry, swayed to and fro for a moment with his hood ominously raised, then turned and glided away, greatly to my relief, whereupon the frog jumped down from his sanctuary. "How wonderful he is!" I thought, "the weakest thing would be safe with him," and indeed no creature ever appealed to my father's pity in vain.

My mother loved Sadhankanan, and I remember how pretty she used to look among those beautiful surroundings. She was small, with tiny hands and feet and a wealth of dark hair, and she had a lovely voice which was heard to the best advantage in our hymns and Bengali songs. Mother's gentle influence kept us very much together. She was a woman of strong convictions, and would never countenance anything which her conscience told her was wrong. She was a charming story-teller, and would often tell us fairy tales when we were in bed. We loved these stories and never wearied of listening to them; some of them I have collected together in a little volume, and one I will include here.

A Maharajah had two wives, and he loved the second far more than the first. Yet the first wife was lovely, gentle, unselfish, and kind-hearted, and the second was just the reverse; she was haughty, vain, ill-tempered, and very jealous of the first wife. The first wife had a baby boy, the heir, to whom the Maharajah was very devoted, and much to the annoyance of the second wife he often played with the baby, who was just beginning to crawl. One day, while he was playing with the child, he sang to him over and over again: "I love this face with its toothless smile," and the second wife hearing, could not get the expression out of her head, "toothless smile." The next time the Maharajah came to see the second wife he found her crawling on the floor, and thought she had gone mad. He asked her what she was doing, and when she opened her mouth to answer he saw, to his horror and disgust, that she had no teeth. "What have you done to yourself?" he asked angrily. She answered him with a hideous smile, "Did you not say to your baby that you loved the face with a toothless smile?" With a furious look he said, "Begone, you are no longer my wife. Your insane jealousy banishes you for ever from the palace;" and weeping and lamenting, she was turned away.

My mother lived for my father and his beliefs. The world never troubled her. "You cannot impede my work, for it is God's work," were the words which formed the keynote of my father's steadfast faith, and my mother accepted it with perfect conviction. She never seemed distressed by her loss of caste, although she was left out of many a family gathering in consequence. I think my mother, however, sometimes pitied us, for we shared her fate when festivities took place in the old house, and she then made much of us in her gentle way. But we led our lives secure in the belief that the religion practised by my father was the highest. His life and his teachings were so beautiful that it was impossible not to try and live up to his ideals, and his yoke was so light that we never felt it.

In the days of my youth, as well as at the present time, I found the greatest consolation in religion. Not the fierce fanaticism which scourges the trembling soul, not the appeal of beautiful music and gorgeous vestments which attract the eye and drug the heart, but the simple and direct appeal to God as a father and a friend, the close and perfect understanding between the Creator and His creature.

We children loved the religious services, and the remembrance of my father's face as he prayed often comes back to me. I have another vivid memory of those days: sometimes, long before the servants were awake, a beautiful voice filled the dawn with melody. It was one of my father's missionaries who, alone upon the roof, sang the praise of God in that sweet and silent hour. I can hear the echo of his song even now. We children used to think that we were very near to heaven then, and we secretly imagined that the singer was an angel visitant.

We were kept quite apart from the world, and light talk and unkind gossip were things unknown to us. Some of my readers may think that I must have led a dull kind of life. Possibly I did in the eyes of the world, but it was happiness to me. As for clothes, we were content with our ordinary muslin saris, and did not see the beauty of foreign goods.

We are very hospitable in the East. In our home, if unexpected guests arrived, mother would say to us girls, if we were at home in the holidays, "Go and take what is wanted out of the store." One would cut the vegetables, and dear mother would cook, and within a short time quite a good meal would be prepared. There is such a nice word used in the Indian housekeeping world, "bart-auta," which means "end to an increase"; we never say: "there is none," or "it is finished." The stores should never be empty, but the new supplies come in before the old are finished.

I was always very much attached to my eldest brother, Karuna. I called him "Dada" (elder brother); he and I were great friends. I remember that once a fine idea struck him. "Let's make soap," he said; "everybody uses soap, and there is a lot of money in it. Sunity, we will become very rich."

My youngest uncle (my mother's brother) was asked to be a partner in the scheme, and we collected quantities of lime, oil, and essences wherewith we thought to produce the ideal cleanser. These we heaped anyhow into a frying-pan and began to heat them up. But to our dismay we found something was wrong. The smoke and flames nearly blinded us, and we were forced to retreat and let the horrid mess burn itself out.

Coolootola was our playground, and I think if the walls could have spoken to us they might have related some very strange stories of the old doings at "Sen's House." I always felt the rooms had histories, and I remember a certain staircase which report said was haunted, and which was the scene of two uncanny happenings when I was a child. Once when my cousins were playing hide-and-seek, one of them seemed to be held back by some unseen force as he ran down the staircase. When at last he managed to shake off the terror which possessed him, he fainted.

I was equally frightened at the same place, but in a different way. My father always cooked his own breakfast, and it was a great privilege to me in my holidays to be allowed to help him. One day he had finished his breakfast, and I was bringing away the curry which was left, and walking very carefully down the staircase, my thoughts set on the dish I was holding, when suddenly I had the impression that a whole army of cats was after me. I looked back. There was nothing to be seen. I went on, and again the feeling of being stealthily followed came over me; I felt I was in the midst of furry, wicked-eyed creatures, and almost heard their velvety paddings around me. I was suffocated with the presence of cats, and dreaded the spring which I felt every moment they would make. Shaking with terror, I kept myself from dropping the dish only by a great effort.

Once when we were playing, my sister Bino and I were left on the roof. I was like a boy, and ran and jumped, and I said to Bino, "I shall run down the stairs much faster than you can, and you will be left alone in the middle of the haunted staircase." Poor Bino looked alarmed, she was slim and delicate; she began to run, but long before she reached the terrace I got there and closed the door, expecting her to cry or try to push the door, but nothing happened, and I got so frightened I flung open the door. There was no Bino to be found. I had a fright. I ran up and down the stairs several times and searched the enormous roof above, but could not find her. I felt something must have happened to Bino, as "the ghost lives in the staircase." I cried a great deal, and then walked slowly down to the bedroom verandah feeling miserable and most ashamed of myself. There I found Bino looking quite happy, and instead of scolding me she said in her sweet way, "I went downstairs when I found the door closed." It was a greater punishment than if she had scolded me.

My brothers and sisters have all followed my father's teachings throughout their lives. I am sure there is not one of that happy band of children who played about "Sen's House" who has not found the greatest comfort and support from our upbringing. My eldest brother, in particular, was very religious, and carried on my father's work, helped by his wife, who copied many of my father's prayers and taught in the Victoria College when it needed teachers.

My second brother, Nirmal, is a most amiable and easy-going man. He is now in the India Office in London and works hard for the welfare of Indian students in London, a subject upon which he has very decided ideas. He is very popular, always ready to help others, and is very happy in his home life. He married a Miss Luddhi.

My third brother, Profullo, was wonderfully gifted. He was a most affectionate little friend to me when I was a bride in the big house in Calcutta, and was almost always with me. On several occasions when I went to England with my children, and my dear husband could not go, Profullo went instead and managed everything. He was my children's favourite uncle.

A wonderful thing happened to Profullo when he was a few weeks old. He fell ill, and the doctors gave him up; at the time my father was away at Belghuria garden-house, and the sad news had to be sent to him. When at length my father arrived every one was weeping, thinking the boy was gone. My father entered the room with a lovely rose in his hand, and they all saw what a wonderful expression there was upon his face. Father touched Profullo's face with the flower, and the boy opened his eyes and said, "Father, have you come?" and from that day he rapidly recovered. Profullo had several pet names, Pepery, Peter, and Pip and Peroo.

He married an English girl. He was always a devoted follower of my father's.

My husband used to say that my father's great gifts and devoutness were inherited by my fourth brother, Saral. Every one thought he would become a missionary. When he was a small boy, he always said he would carry on my father's work. He is unselfish, most kind-hearted and simple minded. His pet name is Bhopal.

My youngest brother's name is Subrata, and his pet name is Bhajan. He was my eldest son's best friend: the boy was devoted to him and asked for him till the end. Subrata is now a doctor, yet we still regard him as our baby brother, and I do not think he will ever grow up; he behaves like a baby. He married a pretty French girl and did well during the War, although I am sorry to say he did not obtain a permanent post.

My sisters are the dearest of women. The second, Savitri, is quiet and retiring, with many good qualities. Her pet name is Bino. She is a tall, handsome girl, the best of wives, and a very good mother. She married a cousin of my husband's, and it has been a great happiness and comfort to me to have her with me all these years in Cooch Behar, where we have worked hand in hand.

My third sister, Sucharu, is most unselfish, and her experiences have made her more than usually sympathetic with the sorrows of others. She was engaged when quite a girl to the Maharajah of Mourbhanj, but his family came between them and he married a Hindu girl.

My sister suffered for several years, as it is an unknown thing for an Indian girl to be an "old maid," and we were disappointed, annoyed, and distressed that such trouble had befallen her. But my sister loved the Maharajah just the same all through, and never said an unkind word. "It is my fate, don't blame him," she said.

We tried to persuade her to marry, but nothing would induce her to forget her lover. Fourteen years passed, during which she was an angel in our house. Then she found her long-delayed happiness. The Maharajah's wife died, and he came back to ask my sister to marry him. The marriage took place in Calcutta, and for some time the Maharajah and my sister led the happiest of lives. But Fate, mysterious Fate, ordained that Death, which had given them happiness, should destroy it. The Maharajah was accidentally shot at a shooting party, and my sister's life was darkened for ever.

She lives for her children and for her stepsons. Some English ladies once said to me that they had no idea the Maharajah had any children by his first marriage, as the whole family seemed so united and devoted to the Maharani.

My fourth sister, Monica, who is very handsome, prayed that luxury might never come into her life for fear the world should make her forget God. We call her Moni; she has the most happy, contented disposition imaginable. No one has ever heard her utter an unkind word. She takes everything as it comes, quietly and without complaint, and thinks herself the happiest woman in the world. Her faith in God is wonderful. She married a Professor in the Education Department, a very clever man, whose name is Sadhu Mahalanobis.

Sujata, the youngest, has always made sunshine in our midst. She is as sweet as some lovely flower, and I think her one idea is to give every one as much pleasure as she can. She was so pretty that when our present King as Prince of Wales lunched with us he asked, "Who is that very pretty girl in the sari?" Sujata married a Mr. Sen, brother of my fourth sister-in-law.

How happy we were! I think that Providence always gives us compensations for our sorrows. There are some hours the glory of which triumphs over the darkness which later clouds our lives: some loved voices whose sweet remembrance deadens the sound of unkind tongues: some faces that in our memory have always a loving smile.

I am happy and proud to say that my brothers and sisters have always been most kind and loving to me.

I was not considered a pretty child, but I remember that a great-uncle once said to my mother: "This little girl, Sunity, will be somebody one day, for I see a lotus in her eyes." "I shall have a handsome son-in-law," my mother laughingly replied, and I was greatly amused. When I was twelve I thought I would make a vow never to marry. My ambition was to be clever, to travel a great deal, and to be a sort of nun. I asked a school friend of mine named Kamari if she also would promise not to marry. To my great disappointment she said: "It is too hard a vow to take," but added affectionately, "we will try." Once some of the nuns from Loretto Convent visited my father's school, and one of them, looking at me gently, asked: "Would you like to be a nun?" We frequently visited this convent, and the kind nuns often came to see us. I admired and loved those nuns.

Even now whenever I get an opportunity I go to see the Convent Sisters.

Chapter III

FESTIVALS AND FESTIVAL DAYS

Many of our customs are full of colour and life, but few people of the West realise their inner and more sacred meanings. By the foreigner we are regarded more often than not as picturesque figures with a background of elephants, tigers and temples, and the poetry of our mythology is missed by the globe-trotter and the official. I have heard Lakshmi the Luck-bringer described as "odd-looking," Kali as a "monstrosity," and the figure of Ganesh as "an extraordinary-looking image." Symbolism is not understood by those people who call our jewels "bits of glass," and our gold "brassy." I wish I could make Europeans realise how proud India is of her women, and how well they have merited her pride. Perhaps few of my readers know any of the stories of the devotion of mothers and wives which is shown daily in the shadow of the purdah.

"Oh, but you ladies can't really know what love means," once remarked a pretty Englishwoman. This sweeping statement is about as absurd and false as the Maharajah of musical comedy or the Anglo-Indian novel, but like most absurdities it has been taken seriously, with the result that many Englishwomen have no idea of the love that exists between Indian wives and their husbands.

One of my cousins married a rich young man when she was quite a little girl. After a few years he died leaving no child. The young widow went back to her mother and lived the life of a poor woman in her father's house. She only ate one meal of vegetables at mid-day. During the cold months a single blanket was her only covering, and in the hot weather she slept upon a coarse mat.

She prayed for hours. She was lovely to behold and her sweetness made her beloved by every one. Yet, from sheer devotion to her husband's memory, this delicately brought up girl chose to lead the life of a servant. It was her tribute to him, the offering of herself.

The question will naturally arise as to what good resulted from this penance, but it proved (according to her views) my cousin's love for her husband, and it showed that she lived up to the traditions of wifely devotion which are taught us from our infancy.

Every province has its own marriage customs, and child marriages in Bengal are still most picturesque, although I am sorry to say that some of the pageantry and the tender sentiment associated with it, is gradually disappearing. A girl is always married in the home of her parents, and she fasts the whole day. In the evening married ladies dress the little bride artistically in new clothes and new jewellery. The air is sweet with perfumes. Flowers are everywhere. The murmur of many voices rises and falls, and suddenly the conch shells are sounded by the ladies of the house, announcing the arrival of the bridegroom.

What a supreme moment for the little bride! Her heart beats fast beneath the stiff golden embroideries, and the new jewellery suddenly becomes as heavy as lead. "What will he think of me?" Anxious and perplexed she goes through the Vasan ceremony, which is performed by the ladies in the courtyard; but she is keenly alert when she is placed on a piece of wood and, thus seated, is carried by young relations and friends to meet her lord and master. The procession passes round the bridegroom and the bearers hold the bride up in front of him. A scarf is thrown over the pair and their eyes meet for the first time.

The marriage is not concluded until the morning of the second day, when the bridegroom takes the bride to his father's house, and this affords an opportunity for the hospitality the Indian delights to show. For a mile or two the route taken by the wedding procession is sometimes sprinkled with rose-water, and the lights flash. "It is a son who is getting married," says the proud father, and he remembers with satisfaction that this home-coming has been fixed for a lucky day and a lucky hour. The bride must also be lucky, for does she not walk gently and speak gently? And is not her forehead of the right shape? Certainly she has not the prominent forehead that brings bad luck.

When the bride arrives at her future home, her husband's sisters throw water and money under the palki, and the jewel-covered little girl is lifted out by her mother-in-law and placed upon a large plate filled with milk and alta (a sort of rose-coloured confection), upon which she stands until the marriage ceremony is over. Then the newly-married couple sit upon a new cloth and receive presents and blessings from the bridegroom's friends and relations.

"May you speak like honey," whispers a maiden as she touches the pretty lips of the bride with honey. "May you hear sweetness like honey," she continues, as she drops honey into the small ears. Then the bridegroom's mother comes forward, gives the bride a pair of bangles and lifts the head-dress which hides her face. As she does this the guests have an opportunity of seeing the blushing little face, and begin to praise her looks, the mother-in-law meanwhile saying, "This is my Lakshmi" (goddess of luck).

On the third day gifts arrive from the bride's father: gifts of jewels, dresses, sweets, scents, soaps—sometimes to the number of five hundred or a thousand. Porters bring them in and the bride and bridegroom change into the new robes. This ceremony is called the Feast of Merriment, for everyone is gay. On the third evening there is another ceremony called the "Fullsaya" (flower ceremony), when the bride is adorned with flowers and the rooms are filled with them. The meaning of this is: Nature with flowers comes to bless the newly united couple.

We thought more of New Year's Day than Christmas Day, probably because that was my father's custom. On New Year's Day we gave each other presents, had dinner parties and sent sweets, fruits, and vegetables to friends. Since we lost my father we have regarded New Year's Day as of more importance than ever, because it is the day on which he opened the Sanctuary at Lily Cottage and preached there his last sermon.

We have a festival which is sometimes held in February, sometimes in March, according to the moon, called "Hooly." It was founded in honour of the Hindu god Krishna, and is one of the most enjoyable days in a Hindu household. Buckets and huge tumblers are filled with rose-water which is coloured with red powder. Then the ladies in all the different courtyards load syringes with the red liquid and, singing and dancing, maid and mistress, old and young, relations and friends, squirt each other amid screams of delight. Afterwards presents of garments are made all round, for the old saris are stained with red. The servants who cannot play put a little red powder on their master's and mistress's feet. This festival is known as the Merry Festival.

In India, religious festival days are chiefly distinguished by their entertainments. My readers will perhaps be surprised at this, but it is true. On festival days banana trees are placed on each side of the house door, and, at the foot of the trees, large earthern pitchers filled with water, and a big cocoa-nut. These are the lucky signs denoting an auspicious occasion. A band plays during the whole of the festival. Every one's house is open to rich and poor. Every one receives presents, often very valuable, and no one is too poor to receive something.

Some years ago a poor Brahmin wanted to have durga puja; he was so poor that he had to beg from door to door in order to get a little money to buy the puja articles and to entertain at breakfast and dinner the people who came to see the goddess. This time he could only obtain very little money, but still he invited a small number of guests and when they arrived they were surprised to find the goddess not properly dressed. "How is it," they asked severely, "that the goddess is left like this?" The poor Brahmin said: "I am a poor son of my Mother, and my Mother knows it; I haven't money with which to dress her. The little I had I used to entertain my guests; if I had had more I would have invited more guests."

There is another festival in India called "Bhaikota," which is held in the autumn, in October or November, and is in honour of brothers. Early in the morning sisters bathe, put on new saris and wait for their brothers. When the brothers are seated, their sisters take small cups of sandalwood paste and with their little fingers put small paste marks on the foreheads of their brothers, saying, "As I put this mark on my brother's forehead may there be no thorns at the door of

Death. As Death is deathless, may my brother be deathless." When the sisters say these words the conch shells are blown, and they give presents to their brothers, and to their cousins, generally of clothes. This ceremony is to show what a heavenly relationship there is between a brother and a sister. The younger sister touches the feet of the elder brother, and the elder sister puts her hands on the younger brother and blesses him.

"Jamai Tashti" is the name of a ceremony for sons-in-law. The wife's parents invite their sons-in-law to their house and the mother-in-law, in a long head-dress, brings presents and puts them in front of the sons-in-law. It is a great day for the younger brothers- and sisters-in-law, they are full of tricks.

I remember once, with some of my girl friends, playing tricks on our cousins-in-law. We made a dish of straw and prepared betel-leaf with all sorts of rubbish, such as peelings of nuts, etc., and the cousins had to eat it, as if they give in or say anything it means that they lose and others gain.

Between April and May there is a great festival, called "Poonyah" (the Day of Good Luck). On this day the Maharajah sits on the throne, and all the high officials, the jemindars and the heads of the districts come. It is a grand sight; the Maharajah in his gold-embroidered robes, and all the men in their State garments. The Dewan of the State sits opposite the Maharajah and on either side of him, covered with cloth, are two pitchers in which the money is put. In front are lights in little earthern vessels. After the Maharajah has taken his seat all the landlords and officials present their tribute in little bundles, which are handed to the Dewan, who puts them into the pots. Music is played the whole time outside. Then the personal staff offer His Highness attar, and flowers and betel-leaf, in golden vessels, making the same offering afterwards to the princes and to the Maharajah's wife and mother, after which the same offerings are made in silver vessels to the officials and landlords. My husband was, I think, the only Maharajah who never had nautch girls or actresses at his Court, and the ladies of the palace always sat in the balcony screened off. After the ceremony was over we had musical parties, or open-air theatricals known as jatras, but there were no actresses in them.

Later on, when my husband had this festival, my four handsome sons, three in their Indian costumes and Rajey in the Royal Yeomanry uniform, looked fine. After the official tributes had been offered the four boys went up the steps of the throne on which their father was seated and with bent heads paid their homage, and my husband put his hand on each son's head in turn and blessed him. Some English people who were present on one of these occasions said they had never seen anything so attractive and so touching.

Chapter IV

MY ROMANCE

My happy home life continued undisturbed until I was thirteen. Indian girls of that age are more advanced than their Western sisters, but I was still very much a child, thanks to my parents.

My father's name is for ever associated with the Civil Marriage Act, as it was entirely owing to his exertions that the Government passed this wise measure fixing the marriageable age of men and girls at eighteen and fourteen respectively.

The fairy prince in my romance was the young Nripendra Narayan Bhup Bahadur, Maharajah of Cooch Behar, who had been a ward of the Government since his infancy, and carefully educated to be a model ruler. Colonel Haughton wrote: "Ever since I have become Commissioner for Cooch Behar, the honour of the young Maharajah, his future happiness, and the welfare of the State have been my anxious care."

This Indian prince's family records show that he was descended from one of the oldest ruling families in the country. According to popular tradition his race had been founded by the love of a god and a maiden, and through successive ages strife and love have been associated with the dynasty of Cooch Behar, whose chiefs are always great rulers, great lovers, and great fighters.

The first wish of the Government was to prevent any palace interference with the baby Maharajah's upbringing. When his father, the late Maharajah, was a ward of the Government, the Maharanis had been very hostile to the idea of a foreign education, and similar opposition was what the Government now wanted to avoid. Therefore, for this and other private reasons which can easily be understood when it is remembered that the late Maharajah left many wives, the Maharajah was removed, when he was five years old, to the Wards' institution at Benares, near which the members of the Cooch Behar Raj family lived in several houses known as the Cooch Behar Palace.

When he was eleven, the Government removed him from Benares to Patna, where he became a student at Government College, and Colonel Haughton's anxious instructions to Babu Kasi Kanto Mukerji, who was in charge of the boy, were "to watch over his conduct and the management of the household: to see that strangers and unauthorised persons have no access to them: and generally to discharge such duties with regard to him as a good parent is bound to do."

In 1872 Mr. St. John Kneller became his tutor and guardian. The Maharajah remained in Patna for five years, during which time he and Mr. Kneller visited the North-Western Provinces, Oudh, and the Punjab, and in 1877 the Maharajah attended the Durbar at Delhi, when the Queen was proclaimed Empress of India. The Viceroy, the late Lord Lytton, received the young ruler most cordially, and presented him with the Kaisar-i-Hind medal. Now for the first time the Maharajah was saluted with thirteen guns, and had a European guard of honour to attend him.

So far the experiment of training the ideal ruler for the ideal state had succeeded beyond the highest expectations of the Government. The Maharajah had become a clever young man and a keen sportsman and, as Mr. Dalton remarked at the Chaurakaran ceremony at Cooch Behar in 1876, "His Highness is fond of his native soil and the people, and enjoys himself thoroughly, taking an interest in everything."

But now arose the question of the future. To ensure final success for the Government's scheme, it was necessary that the young ruler should marry an equally advanced girl, who would second him in his (and incidentally the Government's) efforts for Cooch Behar.

The difficult problem then arose as to whether an educated wife would agree to the polygamy hitherto customary with Maharajahs, and to adopt the many old-fashioned ideas and ways of a Hindu Court. The Government was keenly alive to the fact that marriage might make or mar their experiment, and they were determined to do all they could to prevent failure.

But as it is a principle of the British not to interfere with the marriage question in India, it was necessary for them to be very discreet in their plans, which required great tact to carry out with success.

Mr. Jadab Chandra Chuckerbutty, the Magistrate of Cooch Behar, was deputed to make confidential investigations and find if possible the enlightened girl whom the Government could approve as the Maharani of Cooch Behar. He carried out his mission with discretion; but none of the girls whom he found came up to the required standard.

It was absolutely necessary for the question of the Maharajah's marriage to be settled without further delay, as his visit to England was in contemplation. This journey was a very sore point with the Palace ladies, and Sir Richard Temple, then the Lieutenant-Governor of Bengal, had discussed it rather heatedly.

"During my interview with the Rajah's mother and grandmother," wrote Sir Richard, "these ladies expressed anxiety regarding the Rajah's visiting England, which they deprecated on the grounds that after seeing Europe he would never care for such a place as Cooch Behar nor for such quiet, homely people as his relatives. I explained that it had not been decided whether the Rajah should visit England; but that, if he did, it would only be for a short time, enough indeed to enlarge and strengthen his mind, but not enough to make him forget his home and kindred; and that, while giving him the benefit of an English education, we should take every pains to train and prepare him for the duties he would hereafter have to discharge as the head of a Hindu State."

These arguments somewhat pacified the ladies, but they maintained that only as a married man could the Maharajah go away from India with any degree of security. At that time they had not realised that the hope of the Government was that the Maharajah would take one wife only when the time for his marriage came.

The party from Cooch Behar in search of a bride at last arrived at Calcutta, and Mr. Chuckerbutty went direct to Prosonna Babu, one of my father's missionaries, for advice and help. After several interviews and discussions Jadab Babu spoke of me. But Mr. Chuckerbutty said: "It is too much to expect that the Minister's daughter will be our Maharani;" still they thought they would try.

When the marriage was first suggested my father was very surprised. He never gave a thought to worldly or family affairs; his mind was too full of his religious work; and he refused the offer. But the Government and the representatives of the State would not be discouraged. They continued writing to my father, interviewing him, and sending messages urging that the marriage of the young Prince and myself was most desirable. My father repeatedly refused. In one of his letters he said that I was neither very pretty nor highly educated, and therefore I was not a suitable bride for the young Maharajah.

This unexpected opposition was a set-back to the plans of the Government, and they determined it must be overcome at any cost. Those in authority were clever enough to understand that they must discover my father's weak point and work upon it, as it was evident the worldly advantages of the match made no appeal to him.

The messenger went backwards and forwards several times, for Jadab Babu and others would not hear of any refusal. My father with a troubled mind prayed and prayed until at last he obtained light from above and realised that the marriage would be for the spiritual good of the country. Thus he became in the end persuaded that such a union was a Divine command, and if he allowed me to marry this young ruler he would be fulfilling the will of God.

Of course the matter was not mentioned to me, but one day my second sister Bino remarked confidentially: "Father and mother are talking about marriage, aren't they?" "Oh no," I answered; "it's nothing particular, probably one of the young missionaries is going to be married." "Well, let me tell you, it's no missionary, but some one far more important." "It doesn't matter to me," I said, and I thought no more of it.

Later one of the missionaries remarked with meaning in his voice: "You will be surprised in a day or two, Sunity. Some very important people are coming to see the school."

"So much the better," I assured him, "for now you have told me I can study hard and tell the others to do the same."

The day before the officials arrived from Cooch Behar, I fell ill with fever. After a restless night, I awoke to find my father and mother standing by my bedside.

They looked at each other. "Have you told Sunity?" asked my father.

"No," replied mother, "it is better you should."

"Listen, Sunity," said my father. "Has Prosonna Babu mentioned some visitors who are expected to-day?"

"Yes, he said that some Englishmen are coming to see the school; and, father," I faltered, "I can't get up."

"Sunity," answered my father in that loving voice which always made us children thrill with affection, "it is not the school. These gentlemen are coming to see you."

"To see me!" I cried. "Why?" "Sunity," said my father in a gentle voice, "these people are coming to see you, and if we all agree, perhaps some day you will marry a handsome young Maharajah."

I hid my face in my pillow. I could not speak. Marriage was to me an undiscussed subject. I had never considered it. I felt so shy I became quite red in the face.

After a few hours I was told to get ready. Mother gave me some lovely jewels which looked beautiful on my mauve and gold sari. My hair was dressed. We drove over to dear Miss Pigot's school-house, where I usually had lessons. I was very nervous, and through fear and ague combined I trembled like a leaf.

I rested a little while on the verandah. While I was there I was given a strong dose of quinine. I shall never forget the unpleasant taste of that special draught.

Then I was taken to the drawing-room, where Mr. Dalton and the Bengali officials awaited me. Mr. Dalton looked kind but critical.

"Won't you play to me?" he asked.

I obediently seated myself at the piano and played a simple piece of music. Mr. Dalton watched me up to the piano and back to my seat and as I talked to him; and wrote a full description to the young Maharajah afterwards. "Very nice," he said, in such a charming way that I did not think he was examining me. He seemed favourably impressed, and so it proved, for in one of his letters to my father he wrote: "I thought your daughter a very charming young lady, and in every way a suitable bride for the Maharajah."

Letters passed and repassed between Cooch Behar and Calcutta, but nothing was settled until the 27th of January, 1878, when Mr. Dalton wrote as follows:—

"MY DEAR SIR,

"The Lieutenant-Governor has at last decided that the Rajah is to go to England in March, and, looking to the desirability of perfecting his bride's education, it is better that he should be married before he starts. Mr. Eden at first saw difficulties in the way of a match with your family, but our arguments in favour of the proposal have at length found weight with him, and he has given his consent.

"The Rajah has expressed his distaste to being married at all, as I told you in a previous letter, principally because he was averse to being worried about the matter, and partly because he knew that he was not to be permitted to live with his wife at once and wished to remain single until of an age to do so. But he has come to see that an educated bride is not to be procured at all, and is now eager for the alliance with your daughter, the idea of which was always pleasant to him, provided he could secure his mother's consent. This consent I have at length secured with great difficulty, on terms which Babu Jadab Chandra Chuckerbutty will explain to you, and which I hope you will agree to.

"I know it will seem difficult to you to arrange for a wedding on the 6th of March, and also that the idea of marrying your daughter before she has completed her fourteenth year is repugnant to you. But consider the circumstances, and that in fact the marriage will not be a marriage in the ordinary acceptance of the term but a solemn betrothal, the Rajah proceeding to Europe immediately after the ceremony.

"I have read through your memo. There are some paragraphs which I think we can hardly consent to in their entirety, but by a little concession on both sides, I have no doubt that, if you are really well disposed to this marriage, we may come to an agreement which will suit both parties.

"One of the Rani's conditions is that one of your relatives, not yourself, should give away the bride.

"The objection to you is principally based on the fact that you have been to England. I imagine that, as you will be actually present (or may be, if you like), it will not make any great difference to you should a brother or uncle actually repeat the formula. This is a condition on which great stress is laid, and I hope you will not arrest negotiations in limine by refusing to accede to it. Remember that we on our side have had great difficulties to smooth away, and that we have already conceded almost all that we have the power of conceding.

"Remember, also, that if you care about this alliance, it is a question of now or never, for nothing short of the urgency of the case (the Rajah going to England in March and the Ranis in despair at the idea of his going unmarried) would have brought Mr. Eden to change his mind, a thing he rarely does.

"With my regards to yourself, etc."

Observe how in this letter Government smoothed away all my father's objections. The marriage was to be merely a "solemn betrothal," and hey presto! the age difficulty vanished. Concessions were certain so far as his religious scruples were concerned, but the words "now or never" throw a curious side-light upon the Government policy. The Cooch Behar-Sen alliance was necessary to them, and my father was to be finally "rushed" into giving his consent. That such was the case is shown by the following telegram from the Dewan to Babu Chuckerbutty:—

"Deputy Commissioner says can't wait too long even if matter not published. Must have private assurances of Keshub Babu's consent without delay. Remember preparations. 27-1-78."

Then the delight of Babu Chuckerbutty found expression in this letter to Prosonna Babu:—

"MY DEAR PROSONNA BABU,

"Such has been the pleasure of God! and I am amongst you to re-open the question of marriage.

"Mountains and oceans stood as barriers before us, but thanks to the great Remover of all difficulties, we have managed to get over them all.

"Should we not see in all this, the hand of Him who dispenseth of everything human? We have all done all we could: it now rests finally with you as to the remainder. I have just now arrived here. I left Cooch Behar at midnight day before yesterday, and have come in at once. My present address is 6, Bhobani Dutt Lane, and my man will lead you to my house. I hope that our Maharajah is here.

"Yours, etc.,

"JADAB CHUNDER CHUCKERBUTTY."

The Maharajah wrote to my father as follows:—

"MY DEAR SIR,

"I have been asked to let you know what my honest opinion is on the subject of polygamy.

"In reply I beg to inform you that it has always been my opinion that no man should take more than one wife, and I can assure you that I hold that opinion still.

"I give below a statement of my religious views and opinions. I believe in one true God and I am in heart a Theist.

"Yours truly,

"NRIPENDRA NARAYAN BHUP."

Chapter V

MY MARRIAGE

By this time I had become accustomed to talk of my marriage. Often I wondered with mingled fear and pleasure what sort of future was before me. At last a day came when I was to see the Maharajah. As my sister and I waited in my father's room I remember she said: "He is very handsome, so I've been told, and very, very clever."

When the Maharajah arrived we were called into the drawing-room. I was extremely nervous. It had been trying enough to face Mr. Dalton, but I felt more nervous now that the really critical moment had come.

We sat round a big table in the drawing-room. Mr. Kneller came with the Maharajah. They both talked to us for a time. I was so shy I did not know which was the Maharajah and which Mr. Kneller. Presently a man most gorgeously dressed came into the room. He brought something which was placed on the table. After a few minutes my father said: "Sunity, this is a present from the Maharajah to you." I looked up, and as I did so I met the Maharajah's eyes fixed on me full of love, and I blushed. From that moment my future husband and I loved each other. He was so handsome and so charming. He told me afterwards that he had brought the present in his carriage, but wished to see me first, and if he liked me he would offer it, and it would be a token of his love.

We met several times later, but always in the presence of others. Yet I knew the Maharajah loved me.

Notwithstanding our hopes that everything would go smoothly with the preparations, there were constant worries concerning the religious rites. After some weeks, when many messages had passed between the Government, the State, and my father, my sister told me that there was a hitch about the marriage because the State people would not hear of a Brahmo alliance. I answered, "One thing is certain, I shall not change my religion. Yet, Bino, I love the Maharajah and will marry no one else."

More correspondence followed, and at last the priests from Cooch Behar came to our house, and promised my father that the marriage should be arranged as he wished. This was the one thing needful. My father had come to have an affection for the Maharajah. Indeed, the whole of our family had fallen captive to the Maharajah's charm and kindness. He, on his part, clearly liked them all, and had a deep respect and admiration for my father. How well I remember the delightful ceremony of "Jurini" which took place when my marriage was at last settled. On this occasion my fiancé sent saris to all my relations, gave me the most beautiful presents, and distributed more than a hundred plates of sweetmeats, etc., to the household. It was a perfect day, one of those on which it is pleasant to look back and forget in its happy memory the sad events of life.

But the clouds of hostile criticism had been gathering, and at last the storm broke. For some time questions had been asked as to my father's motives in allowing me to be married before the age stipulated in the Act which he had done so much to have passed. My marriage preliminaries were really a stormy time in my life, fulfilling the storm omens at my birth. It is too serious and too long a story to write in this book, but just a few lines may give my readers an idea of what my father had to go through in connection with my betrothal. People who did not have full faith in him and in his doctrines raised unheard-of questions; but the Government was determined on the marriage.

My father could have published the correspondence. He could have explained the situation, but serene in the integrity of his motives, and in his faith in God, he was undismayed by the attacks which were made upon him. His only response was: "I became a Brahmo when I heard the Divine call, and I have given consent to this marriage by the same Divine command. I obey God, not man."

As Miss Pigot wrote almost prophetically: "The generation that were the actors have nearly all passed away, and time will have mellowed these events to the aged survivors. But the new generation, viewing the past in the light of history, will not refuse the crown of martyrdom to the sufferings of Keshub Chunder Sen. It is in the course of human events that by some tragic incident the truest and best men are brought to the slaughter."

Having achieved their end and obtained my father's consent to the marriage, it might have been assumed that the Government would have strictly observed their part of the bargain. They had promised to concede everything, and as it was the spiritual side of the ceremony that troubled my father, I think Mr. Dalton ought to have spared him any further worry.

There was one person who was very subtle in his opposition and more powerful than any English official. This was the Dewan, the late Calica Das Dutt, Prime Minister. He was not in favour of the marriage, because he thought he had been ignored. He was an influential follower of my father's, and yet all the correspondence relating to the marriage went through Jadab Babu, who was only a junior officer. His quiet interference is shown in the following letter written by Mr. Dalton to Mr. Chuckerbutty:—

"MY DEAR JADAB BABU,

"The Dewan tells me that he has already written to you regarding my wire as to the extent of Babu Keshub Ghunder Sen's party coming to Cooch Behar for the wedding. Of course, my object is to avoid any unnecessary display of Brahmoism. In marrying a Brahmo girl the Rajah makes a great concession to enlightened ideas, but it is most desirable that this connection should be softened as much as possible in the eyes of his relatives, at Cooch Behar and elsewhere, who are still wedded to the old superstitions, and who would look with horror upon any departure from the old Hindu formula.

"I wish therefore to dissuade Babu Keshub Chunder Sen from bringing with him any of those who might be called his followers, apart from such as are his immediate relatives. In fact, we cannot permit any Brahmo demonstration whatever, and those who come must bear in mind that a single speech in any way whatever relating to Theism versus Idolatry will not be permitted.

"So far as possible, not only Hindu customs, but also the ideas and even the prejudices which arise from these customs must be respected: for instance, I disapprove altogether of the idea of bridesmaids, an idea at once novel and repulsive to strict and bigoted Hinduism. The maiden attendants of the bride should remain in the background and on no account be put prominently forward except when universal custom allows. Also I would suggest that it is quite unnecessary and undesirable that a large company of ladies should accompany the party. I fail to see what good their presence can do.

"I think the ladies should be limited to Keshub Babu's immediate family and one or two intimate friends, and as regards the male guests, please remember that the amount of distinction shown to them here will depend entirely as to their social status in Calcutta, and that only such as are entitled to be admitted and given a seat at the Lieutenant-Governor's Durbars will be considered here.

"Babu Keshub Chunder Sen is too sensible a man not to understand my reasons for all this. Though, of course, I cannot expect him to look at the matter from my point of view.

"It is possible that he may look upon this marriage as the inauguration of a new era in the history of social and religious progress. But in Cooch Behar, at all events, he must wait for the fructification of his work until the Rajah attains his majority.

"Any of the well known and respected members of the Brahmo community who are Babu Keshub Chunder Sen's personal friends, and who would like to come, we will receive with great pleasure, and also any of similar rank and position whom he may wish to bring outside of the Brahmo community. I hold you responsible that a list of the intended party is submitted to me at an early date, to enable me to provide for a special train, etc.; and such list should contain information as to the social status of those composing it.

"You should telegraph to me the number of 1st, 2nd, and 3rd class passengers who will make up the party. It seems to me that there can scarcely be more than twenty, or thirty at the outside, first-class passengers. I have consulted with the Commissioner on this subject, and he agreed altogether with my views.

"Yours sincerely,

"GODFREY T. DALTON."

The final arrangements for our journey to Cooch Behar were left in the hands of Babu Chuckerbutty, and at last everything seemed settled, and we left Calcutta on the 25th February, 1878. We were quite a large party, consisting of my father, mother, grandmother, father's sister, his younger brother, his special followers, two ladies (wives of missionaries), some relations, and a girl friend of mine.

I was naturally very excited, for this more or less State journey was very different from the journeys to which I had been accustomed. It seemed ages before we reached Cooch Behar, by which time the discomforts of the journey had reduced our spirits to zero. I remember how dark the night seemed. We were directed to the house which had been prepared for us, and all of us were delighted to be in a house again. It was comfortably furnished.

Soon after my arrival I asked my sister when I should see the Maharajah, but to my great disappointment I was told that I was not to see him until my wedding-day. The interval was taken up with elaborate ceremonies.

The Dewan and the State officials came to see me. Seated on a carpet, I received them and accepted the coin which tradition demanded they should give, and thanked each by bowing. As I never lifted my eyes, I could not distinguish one from another.

The day before the wedding the Dewan and a few Raj pandits came to see my father and talked over the ceremony. They told him that parts of it would be according to the old Hindu rites. To this my father refused to consent. All these difficulties have been described and explained in books written by missionaries of my father, and I need not repeat them here.

The town was beautifully illuminated and decorated. I felt very nervous, though very happy at the thought of seeing my betrothed. When the time drew near, I was sad at the thought of leaving the home that had been such a happy one.

To our great surprise the time appointed for my departure passed, and there was no sign of my going away. Then we heard that the State officials were still discussing the question whether we should be married before the Maharajah left for England or after his return.

After a long delay I was told to get ready. They dressed me in a pretty sari and I was soon ready to go. My sister Bino and I went in one palki, and my grandmother followed in another. A grand escort from the palace came to fetch me. The time to say good-bye had now come. I touched my father's and mother's feet, and said good-bye to the others. I realised that I was bidding farewell to my childhood, and that I stood on the threshold of a new life quite different from anything I had ever imagined. The thought frightened me, and I broke into loud sobs.

As in a dream I heard my father's beautiful voice comforting me. His tender words fell like balm on my aching heart. He whispered one short sentence which gave me strength for my ordeal.

I dried my tears. Then, accompanied by my sister and followed by my grandmother, I went to my future home. Never shall I forget that journey through the crowded streets. I could hear the outcry which greeted our palkis. The torches flashed with a weird effect. At last the palkis stopped in the courtyard of the zenana part of the Cooch Behar palace.

I found myself in the midst of a great crowd of women. I stood, the observed of all, and listened to the various comments on my appearance. I was outwardly calm, but in reality I was a very scared miserable little girl. Then a lady came forward bearing lights and flowers. It was the Maharajah's mother, and she was performing Varan, or welcoming the bride.

After the Varan the crowd of women made way for us and we were taken to a reception-room. I was nervous and tired and longing for a rest, when suddenly I heard a gentle whistle outside. It was the Maharajah! I knew his whistle well, for I had often heard it at Lily Cottage. I felt at once that I was not forgotten, that in the darkness there was a cheery companion who loved me and wanted my love. I would have answered back in sheer joy, but could not. My sister and I were soon in bed. She immediately fell into the healthy sleep of tired youth, but I was too fatigued and nervous, with a thousand and one thoughts worrying me, to be able to sleep.

The next morning we were up early. It was my wedding day, and I had to go through a good deal before the ceremony. After my bath, my grandmother was told that a Hindu priest wished to recite the usual prayers. When we came out on the verandah, we saw the Brahmin waiting surrounded by relations of the Maharajah. Some one put a gold coin into my hand which I was requested to give to the priest of the Raj family.

My grandmother interposed. "No, no," she said, "our girls don't do this."

"What nonsense!" replied the Maharajah's grandmother. "Why! it means nothing."

But we were firm, and I placed the coin on the floor. This was only one of the petty annoyances which occurred during the day.

In the evening of the marriage the Maharajah's mother came and spoke to my mother most harshly. One of her remarks I still remember: "Do you mean to say you love your daughter? How can you when you do not wish her to marry a Maharajah? If she does not marry my son according to Hindu rites, she will not be the Maharani."

My mother answered gently but very firmly: "I shall be sorry if my daughter does not marry your son, and I shall take her away from Cooch Behar; but my daughter shall never marry any one according to Hindu rites." This made the Maharajah's mother furious.

While these disputes and discussions were going on in the palace, my dear father must have suffered a great deal silently in his house. There was much hot argument. Both sides were obstinate. Telegrams were dispatched to Government. Cooch Behar waited. Sunset came. It was the auspicious hour fixed for the marriage, but no word went forth that it was to take place.

Gradually silence reigned. The music and the sound of the conch shells ceased. The voice of the crowd was hushed. All of a sudden everything stopped. The musicians left the platforms and the town became perfectly quiet; the illuminations were extinguished one by one.

Then the unexpected happened, and the Gordian knot of caste and creed was suddenly cut. The news of the final dispute had been conveyed to the Maharajah. When he realised that the religious obstacles might prove insurmountable he became so strangely quiet and serious that his people felt rather nervous and wondered what their young master would do. He took very strong measures.

Looking at those near him, with determination in every line of his set young face, the Maharajah, said: "Now give good heed to my words. I am going to bed. If I am to marry this girl, wake me up. Otherwise have my horse in readiness, for I shall ride away from Cooch Behar for good and all to-morrow morning. If I cannot marry this girl, I will marry no one."

A great hush fell on those who heard, and there was general consternation. Never before had Nripendra Narayan Bhup so asserted himself. His councillors saw that their ruler intended to have his own way.

It was now midnight. My father was alone in his quiet house, as one and all had left for the palace. His soul was far beyond all earthly things, for he communed with the God who had never forsaken him. I believe that in that solemn hour he found the peace so healing to his soul.

Suddenly the sound of carriage wheels broke the stillness of the night. Steps hurried up the stairs. The door was flung open, and Mr. Dalton, pale and breathless, stood before my father.

"Mr. Sen," he cried, "the wedding must and shall take place to-night. The service shall be exactly as you wish. I'll be there to see that it is not interfered with. Come quickly. We've not a moment to lose. There is another auspicious hour at 3 a.m. Let it be then."

As he spoke he handed my father a written agreement confirming his words, and told him that the Lieutenant-Governor had telegraphed: "Let the marriage be performed according to the rites as settled in Calcutta."

Mr. Dalton almost dragged my father to the waiting carriage, and followed by some of our friends they made their way with difficulty through the crowded streets.

Then as in a fairy tale the scene changed. The stillness was broken by music. The darkness was flooded with light. The whole town was illuminated in an instant; the band played, the conch shells sounded, fireworks were sent up. All was joyous and brilliant.

Our wedding was celebrated in an enormous tent: the crowd remarked that I looked very nice in a pale blue sari with raised gold flowers worked upon it and a bright red satin veil with masses of gold, the creation of a French dressmaker. But I felt very nervous when, seated on a piece of wood, I was carried between lines of soldiers, the Maharajah following close behind.

He was like a wonderful picture, one mass of gold from head to foot, and the shimmering fabric seemed moulded to his fine figure. I went through the ceremony with perfect confidence. The service was performed by the Rev. Gour Govind Roy, who was one of the staunchest missionaries of our Church, and all the Maharajah's Hindu priests were also present.

It was lovely to think that we belonged to each other from that day, and I was so happy. Certainly never did any girl possess a more perfect husband than the Maharajah. He was so full of tender thought, and he planned most exciting surprises in the shape of lovely gifts for me.

But the next few days were very trying. The palace ladies used to threaten and scold me by turns. "You must become a Hindu," was their incessant, wearying refrain, and I was heartily glad when the time came for me to return to Calcutta.

My husband had already gone to Darjeeling with Mr. Dalton, to interview the Commissioner before his departure for England.

We left Cooch Behar without regret. Great was my joy and surprise to find that the Maharajah had arranged to join our train and travel part of the way with us. Soon after our arrival in Calcutta he left for England, and I fell to wondering whether the past few weeks had been a dream or not.

Chapter VI

EARLY MARRIED DAYS

After we returned from Cooch Behar I found (although I understood little about such serious matters then) that most of my father's followers had raised objections to my marriage. But I believed that nothing could hurt my father and that no one could do him harm.

These people continually attacked him and plotted to undermine his authority. The fire of discontent and disloyalty which they kindled blazed fiercely and dazzled the eyes of the unfaithful. Some of them even went so far as to threaten to kill him. All those who had feeble faith left our Church, one after another. Even this did not satisfy the malcontents, and they built a church of their own which is known as Sadharan-Somaj. One of their members, who is now dead, published a book called "The History of the Brahmo-Somaj." I do not wish to discuss the subject, but I may say this book plainly shows that not only the man who wrote it was in the wrong, but all the members of his Church. They are all responsible for preaching untruths. I have learned from my babyhood that truth conquers untruth. Yet it is sad to think that educated and enlightened men should allow such books to be published. I am waiting for some dutiful son of the Church of the New Dispensation to write the true history of the Brahmo-Somaj. I hope that the members of the Sadharan-Somaj do not think we do not believe in our doctrine of Universal Love. If they would accept the truth of the New Dispensation they would find us waiting to welcome and love them as brothers and sisters. It is sad that followers should work against their leader, their preacher, their minister, and persist in making the gulf wider every day.

Many of my father's followers insisted that my marriage had been a Hindu ceremony. Yet it was not an idolatrous one, and I often wonder why the Government never publicly defended my father and declared the truth. For the Government was most anxious for the Maharajah to marry me, and could easily have made the case clear to the public. They also might have spoken for my father, as they knew that he was the leader of the Brahmos. However, the marriage was now an accomplished fact, I was Maharani of Cooch Behar, and it was left for me to prove the success or failure of the first Indian marriage which had defied traditional custom.

The public are still uncertain by what rites we were married. The Brahmo Act that my father wished the Government to pass was not agreed to by other Brahmos, such as Maharshi Debendra Nath Tagore, and others. Although the Tagores called themselves Brahmos, they wanted their marriage ceremony to be known as Hindu marriage (non-idolatrous). As they opposed it, the Act was not passed, but instead of it Act III. of 1872, in which one of the many things mentioned was that the bride was not to be under fourteen or the bridegroom under eighteen years of age. But the Brahmo Marriage Bill, as worded by my father and from which the following extract is taken, will remove all misunderstandings:—

"I, A.B., am a native of British India. I do not profess the Christian religion, and I object to be married in accordance with the rites of the Hindu, Muhammedan, Buddhist, Parsi or Jewish religion."

It sounds too dreadful to have to say "No" to all religions. One and all, I believe, resent it, but there is no other law for a Brahmo marriage.

The Maharajah could not be married under this Act as he had his own law in his State, besides he was an independent ruler and a British marriage was of no value in Cooch Behar. Our marriage was recognised by the Government and the State as a Hindu marriage. The Maharajah himself was a Brahmo, but he was the ruler of a Hindu Raj. As we were not married under Act III., the age limit did not affect us.

The following letter, which my father wrote to Miss Cobbe, puts the position clearly.

"Lily Cottage,

"78, Upper Circular Road,

"Calcutta.

"29th April, 1878.

"MY DEAR FRIEND,

"Your kind letter has given me great relief, for which I thank you most sincerely. In the midst of my present trials and difficulties it is truly a Godsend. My antagonists have impeached my character, showered upon me abusive epithets of all kinds, and represented me before the public as one who, for fame and wealth and worldly advantages, has unhesitatingly sold his conscience and his daughter! This is indeed the substance of the charges preferred against me, and an insinuation to this effect is to be found, I am told, in the so-called protest. If my conscience acquits me, none can convict me. Of this I am sure, that I never sought a Rajah. I never coveted filthy lucre. As a private man I should not probably have acted as I have done. I was acting all along as a public man, and one course only was open to me. The British Government sought me and my daughter; a Christian Government that knew me thoroughly to be a Brahmo leader, proposed the alliance, and the weighty interests of a State were pressed upon me with a view to induce me to accept the proposal and make the needful concessions. I found such arguments as these placed before me: 'Here is the Cooch Behar State, a den of ignorance and superstition, with a corrupt Court given to dissipation, polygamy, intrigue, and oppression. The young Rajah has been saved by the British Government acting as his guardian. The women of the Raj family have been mostly removed to Benares, and others will follow. The administration of the affairs of the State has greatly improved in all departments, education, police, revenue, health, etc., under the management of competent officers appointed by the British Government. The new palace will be erected at a cost of about Rs.8,000,000. Not a vestige will remain of the old régime, and the ground will have been thoroughly cleared for political and social improvements when the young Rajah will be formally installed and begin to govern his immense territory. It is desirable, it is of the utmost importance, that he should have an accomplished wife. Should he marry a girl of seven or eight in the old style, the effects of the education he has hitherto received will be neutralised, and he will surely go back into the evil ways from which he has been saved. A good and enlightened wife, capable of exercising always a healthy influence on the Rajah, is the "one thing needful" in the Cooch Behar State.' The Government, in presenting these views before me, seemed to ask me whether I would give my daughter in marriage to the Maharajah and thus help forward the good work so gloriously begun in the State by our benevolent rulers in the interests of millions of the subject population. I could not hesitate, but said at once, under the dictates of conscience, 'Yes.' You have justly said that a grave responsibility would have rested upon me, had I refused the overtures of the Government. In fact, I wonder how you have so clearly realised the position and grasped the real secret of the whole affair. I have acted as a public man under the imperative call of public duty. All other considerations were subordinated to this sacred duty. All other considerations were subordinated to this sacred call, this Divine injunction. I saw, I felt that the Lord had Himself brought before me in the strange ways characteristic of His Providence, the young Maharajah of Cooch Behar for alliance with my daughter. Could I say No? My conscience bade me obey. And there I was, an enchained victim before a strange overpowering dispensation of the living providence of God. I did not calculate consequences, though most beneficial results I could not fail to foresee. I did not go through elaborate logical processes of thought. I did not refer to others for advice, though I saw clearly that the contemplated step involved risks and hazards of a serious character, as the Rajah was an independent chief and might fall back upon the evil customs prevalent in his territory. I trusted, I hoped with all my heart that the Lord would do what was best for me, my daughter, and my country. Duty was mine; future consequences lay in the hands of God. So I acceded to the main proposal of the Government, and negotiations went on between myself and the deputy Commissioners. It was at first proposed that the Rajah should marry under the Marriage Act, and the Government made no objection. I was assured that the Rajah had no faith in Hinduism, but a public renunciation of the Hindu faith was objected to on political grounds. Mr. Dalton wrote to me: 'As a fact, he does not believe in it (Hindu religion), but profession and faith are two different things.' He added, 'These are difficulties, but I think they may be got over, and when you reflect on the benefits to the cause of enlightenment which may result from this marriage, I feel sure you will smooth our way as far as you can, even to the extent of conceding somewhat to Cooch Behar's superstition. The greatest difficulty I see in the way is the public declaration to be made in Cooch Behar by the Rajah that he does not profess Hinduism. If that can be dispensed with, I think other difficulties may be got over. You must remember that Act III. of 1872 does not apply to Cooch Behar, and that there will be nothing illegal in leaving out this part of the programme.' (Deputy Commissioner's letter, dated Calcutta, 24th September, 1877.) Touching the match itself and the question of rites the following occurs in the same letter: 'The Commissioner, Lord Ulick Brown, has written to me expressing his warm approval of the proposed engagement and asking me to obtain from you in writing "what you require," that is to say, to state in writing the points in which the celebration of the marriage must differ from the Hindu ceremony.'"

After my return I resumed my life at Lily Cottage like an unmarried girl, and was not sorry to forget the strenuous days at Cooch Behar. Our home was very peaceful, and as it was half an hour's drive from the town we were right out of the city. Lily Cottage is not isolated now. Houses have sprung up all round it and not many traces of the surroundings of my girlhood remain. It is a large house, with a sanctuary, bedrooms, and drawing-room on the upper story; below is the room that was used by the missionaries, and the dining- and guest-rooms. The grounds were very pretty, and I especially remember the little hut outside where father and the missionaries cooked on Sundays. I used to get up quite early, and take my bath, for I attended to our prayer-room, and it is a strict Brahmo rule that this quiet sanctuary may be arranged only by those whose body and dress are clean. My father plucked flowers from the garden and brought them to the prayer-room every morning, and the service there usually lasted until about half-past twelve. After that I breakfasted and then began my daily lessons.

In India we offer betel leaf if any guest comes, as English people do cigarettes. Our cooks are high-caste, and they have to bathe before they enter the kitchen. One maid goes to the market to buy vegetables, fish, and fruit every morning, other maids have to clean the brass plates, etc., early in the morning; after this they must bathe before they enter any of the rooms in the house. The sanctuary at Lily Cottage is very large; the floor is of marble; and when I went away my mother and sisters used to arrange the flowers. It was wonderful the designs mother made, sometimes from the stars she had seen the evening before. After prayers the children had their breakfast, and then the gentlemen, and then the ladies. Our chief food in India is milk; very little meat is eaten, but plenty of vegetables and fruits in their seasons.

The Government had, according to their ideas, discovered for the ideal wife the ideal governess, a lady of good family, Miss S, a society woman to her finger-tips, but useless except as a teacher of les convenances. I wanted to learn everything possible about the history of other nations, and I was anxious to acquire a good general knowledge of languages. German was the only foreign language which my governess seemed to think necessary for a Maharani; but, as her German was dominated by a strong Scottish accent, I doubted its conversational value. It was an unfortunate experience. No doubt the lady meant well, and regarded me as an uninteresting pupil. But she frightened and repelled me with her trying temper, until I became quite cowed, and my education suffered in consequence. Mrs. White taught me painting, and my sister-in-law taught me Bengali. She was very clever, and the only language I know well is Bengali, thanks to her kind help.

I corresponded frequently with my husband in England; his letters were full of cheery accounts of his visit, and his wish to see me again. He returned to India in February, 1879, and every one was delighted to see how he had profited by his travels. The same year he joined the Presidency College in Calcutta, and lived in a house in Theatre Road. My husband's stay in Calcutta was a time of great happiness for me. He often came to Lily Cottage, where it was decided I should live until he was eighteen, and I was sixteen. He was very fond of my mother, and often teased her about the keys which, according to the Bengali custom, she carried in a knot in her sari. His great delight was to steal these keys and then enjoy her distress when she discovered her loss. "I can't understand why Englishmen hate their mothers-in-law," he said to the English ladies of his acquaintance, "mine is the sweetest imaginable, and I love her as my mother."

The Maharajah and I went to our church regularly every Sunday morning, wet or fine, winter or summer. He respected the missionaries and treated my brothers and sisters as if they were his own, in fact he loved and was beloved by one and all.

The Maharajah was full of praise of England, and there never lived a more loyal subject than he. Indeed, in most ways he was as Western in his ideas as people had anticipated. But he was entirely Indian at heart. The magic of the East held him. The "Land of the Lotus" was his own beloved country. His upbringing never eradicated the strong claims of blood.

When I was sixteen and the Maharajah eighteen it was decided that our "real" marriage should take place in my own dear home. In quiet ways we had gathered the fragrant flowers of friendship's garden, and there we had seen the roses of love which were blooming for us. Our future lay rich and glowing before us, and our happiness was perfect. We were married in the Church of the New Dispensation. How well I remember my wedding morn! As I write I glance at a modest ring, turquoise and diamonds, which never leaves my finger. It was my husband's gift to me on that exquisite day, and I prize it more than all the lovely jewels he delighted to give me.

Every one rejoiced that day. We were like one united family, and I knew that all the good wishes and kind words came straight from the hearts of those present. We started on our new life under the happiest auspices. We left Calcutta by special train in the afternoon for Burdwan, where we were to spend our honeymoon. Our saloon was beautifully decorated with flowers, and a party of friends and relations came to see us off. Just before the train started I pressed my face against my father's arm and had a good fit of sobbing. I knew I was really leaving my childhood's home that day. But when

I found myself alone in the train with my husband a heavenly happiness came over me. We were alone together! We two, who loved each other, and I shall never forget a Bengali song he sang to me that day: "He who has not undergone suffering cannot know love."

At Burdwan we were received in state, and I was treated like a strict purdah lady. The railway station and its approaches were covered in like a huge tent so that no outsiders could catch a glimpse of me, and directly the train stopped a bevy of maidens escorted me to a state carriage. When I was safely on the way to the palace, the draperies were withdrawn and my husband exchanged greetings with the officials who had assembled to offer him their congratulations.

The palace at Burdwan is a splendid building, and our rooms were on a terrace which overlooked the lake. Everything was as romantic as a young girl's heart could desire. But early next morning I was awakened by a dull roar which seemed almost to issue from our rooms. I could hardly believe I was awake until the roar was repeated, and then in an agony of fear I called to my husband: "Oh, do see what is the matter. I believe a tiger is trying to get in." Another roar made me quiver. My husband laughed immensely while he explained that the Maharajah of Burdwan's most cherished possession was a zoological garden which was quite close to our apartments. That was my first tiger experience. I had plenty afterwards at Cooch Behar, and learned that the roar of the tiger in captivity is feeble compared with the majesty of his voice in the jungle where he is king.

One day during our stay at Burdwan I visited the Maharanis, who lived in an old palace. The Dowager Maharani welcomed me cordially and, instead of bestowing the customary present, she filled my hands with sovereigns until I could hold no more. She was a sweet old lady, this Maharani who had given up everything luxurious when she became a widow. She worshipped her late husband's slippers, which she placed before his chair, just as though he were alive and sitting there. I liked the Raj-Kumari, the daughter of the late Maharajah. All the palace ladies were good-looking, and I was struck by the large number of pretty faces.

My honeymoon was a very happy one, but after a few days in Burdwan we returned to Calcutta, and I began to realise the responsibilities of my position as the wife of the Maharajah of Cooch Behar. At first I was not allowed to meet Indian gentlemen, not even my husband's cousins. When English visitors came, I remember one of these cousins throwing their cards through the shutters of my door. Readers may wonder why the Maharajah minded my seeing Indian gentlemen. The good reason was that there were very few Bengali ladies out of purdah in those days, and my husband strongly objected to my meeting men who did not bring out their own wives. Though he was only two years older than me, he was a very strict husband, and I always respected him as if he had been years older; he was my hero and ideal husband, and whatever he said I thought was right. He was very particular about my dress. A lady once remarked: "It is a pity the Maharani doesn't wear her lovely pearls next her skin."

"She is not allowed," the Maharajah answered with a quiet smile.

"Not allowed!" exclaimed the lady, in great surprise. "You surely do not disapprove?"

"Yes, I disapprove."

"But why, Your Highness?"

"Well, simply and solely because I prefer my wife to do what I like. I don't care a bit what other women do."

I don't believe outsiders ever realised how absolutely Indian the Maharajah was at heart, and he had the strictest ideas about my conforming to his ideals. He did not like loud laughter or loud talking. I was not allowed to ride, dance, or play tennis. In later years, when my girls did all these things, he was often asked why he allowed his daughters such privileges.

"I allow Girlie, Pretty, and Baby to be 'outdoor' girls, because I do not know what sort of men they may marry, and if their husbands like these things they will not be found lacking," was his reply.

As I was a Bengali girl and had come from Calcutta, where all my people were, and my husband wished to have a place near, Woodlands was bought and beautifully furnished. I was delighted with my little sitting-room, which was so charmingly decorated in pale pink and blue that it looked like a picture. I still remember some books I had on one table, on cooking, gardening, etc.

There we spent our early married days. Although my husband liked English food, and lived like an Englishman, I was faithful to the Indian cookery with which I was familiar. The hours passed all too swiftly. We began to entertain. I gave two enjoyable dances and believe I was quite a successful hostess.

The Maharajah took great pride in me. "Never forget whose daughter you are," he would say to me, and this appreciation of my dear father touched me very much. Any good I may have done in my life is entirely due to his influence.

In the summer of 1881 I knew I might look forward to the crowning glory of our happiness, for I was expecting to become a mother. Girl though I was, I realised how important a part this child might play in my life at Cooch Behar. For many generations no heir had been born to the ruler's chief wife. The succession had always been through the son of a wife of lower rank. I knew therefore that, if I ever had a son, much of the ill-feeling of my husband's relations towards me would disappear.

A strange thing happened that year, when I was staying up in the hills at Mussoorie. My Indian maid came to me all excitement one morning, saying: "Maharani sahib, there is a fortune-teller outside who wants to see your hand." "Tell him to go away," I said. But the man refused to leave. "Let Her Highness but pick out one grain of rice and send it to me," he urged. So I picked out a grain and sent it to him. I was surprised when the maid returned with the message: "Her Highness will have a son, and he will rule the country." My father also had a premonition about the expected baby. A few weeks before the child arrived, there was a ceremony, and while at prayers, my father said: "A Sebak (a devotee) is coming from God." At times the gift of prophecy is given to men like my father.

In the early morning of the 11th April, 1882, my first son was born at Woodlands. Late at night on the 10th a pandit had read the "Gita," and my relations who were present cried as if I were already dead and gone, as I suffered greatly, and for a couple of hours they did not know if I should survive the birth. But when the baby made his appearance every one exclaimed that his arrival was favoured by the lucky stars then in the ascendant, and still greater was the joy when it was known that the tiny new-comer possessed the "tika" (a prominence on the forehead), which is said to be bestowed only on very powerful rulers.

My father was alone in his room deep in prayer when Mazdidi, my cousin, told him that a prince was born to Cooch Behar. The usual ceremonies took place, and money and sweets were lavishly distributed. But the supreme moment for me was when my husband came into my room and sat by my bedside. "Darling wife," he whispered, "we have a little boy." I looked at him and, though we spoke little, we were so happy. Our thoughts were full of our reward, for our little son was sent by Heaven in recompense for all that we had suffered.

Ah! my darling! My Rajey beloved! you are as near to my heart now in your peaceful paradise as you were on that April morning. You were the fruition of a great love and a perfect faith, but God decreed that your life should be as mutable as your birth month. He bestowed on you all that the world most values. He gave you a beautiful body and a beautiful mind. Yet your days were as a "tale that is told," and the only earthly remains of your beauty and greatness are a few ashes in the rose garden at Cooch Behar.

My father named this child of promise Raj Rajendra (King of kings), but he was always called Rajey. His birth was celebrated with great public rejoicings both at Calcutta and Cooch Behar. On the seventeenth day after the birth, we gave an evening party, when presents were bestowed on the lucky baby, and the whole of Woodlands was illuminated. On another day was the children's festival, when all sorts of pretty things were given to the little visitors, and, in fact, for some time we lived in a perfect whirl of excitement and congratulations.

"Rajey," as we called him, was a perfectly behaved baby, who hardly ever cried, and who was so fair that he was nick-named "the English baby." My husband allowed me to nurse him myself, a privilege not often permitted to Royal mothers.

Every one adored Rajey. Dear old Father Lafont, one of the Jesuit Fathers in Calcutta, always alluded to him as "my boy." We went to Cooch Behar for the naming ceremony, and when I arrived there I found, as I had anticipated, that public feeling had completely changed, and I, as the mother of a Prince, was popular, both in palace and State. There were many palace rules to be followed in regard to the heir; one was that the milk had to be well guarded, and when the cow was milked sentries stood all round her. Some of my happiest days were spent at Simla, and Rajey used often to go and see my father, who had a house there. My youngest brother was only six months older than my boy, so the children were more like playmates than uncle and nephew. Rajey had the simplest upbringing. His rank was never put forward, for it was my husband's wish that his son should be brought up as simply as possible.

On the 31st October, 1883, the Maharajah completed his 21st year, and was installed as reigning ruler on the 8th of November by Sir Rivers Thomson, the Lieutenant-Governor, who made over to him the reins of government. Rajey and his father looked splendid together, and every one congratulated me on having such a handsome husband and such a beautiful son. After a few days in Cooch Behar we returned to Calcutta.

My father had been ailing for a few months; but we little thought that the end of his journey in this world was so near. He had a fine figure, but was much reduced by December, 1883. Still we did not think it possible he would leave us. Nothing I could write would give my readers an idea of how happy our childhood had been. Our home had been for us an abode of "sweetness and light"; and now it was to be shattered by sorrow. To all families such grief must come. To ours, always so united, the shadow of death seemed unthinkable. Yet my father's call had come. On the 1st of January, 1884, early in the morning he expressed a wish to consecrate the new sanctuary in the grounds of Lily Cottage. His physicians and all his relations and followers tried to dissuade him, but he would not listen to them. Though exhausted and very ill, he was carried down to the sanctuary, where he offered his last and most impressive prayers.

On the following Tuesday, the 18th January, just before 10 a.m. my father breathed his last. No one who witnessed it will ever forget the scene at Lily Cottage that morning. The house, the compound, the roads were full of people. The weeping of my mother and grandmother was heartrending. In the first bitterness of my grief I felt that I could never know happiness again. My father's missionaries and followers were like sheep without a shepherd. With him the brightness and joy of our days were gone. My mother gave up everything in the way of comfort. She wore coarse saris, discarded her soft bed and slept on a hard, wooden bedstead. Only the cheapest things were to be seen in her room. But many will have read about this in the Dowager Lady Dufferin's book. Her Excellency was a kind friend to my mother.

My father's ashes rest in a mausoleum built in front of the new sanctuary. The ashes of my mother's body are near his, and close to them the ashes of my brother, his wife and their baby boy, and next to them my third brother, Profulla. It is a peaceful spot, this tomb-house in the garden, and these words of my father are inscribed on his mausoleum:

"Long since has this little bird 'I' soared away from the Sanctuary, I know not where, never to return again.

Peace! Peace! Peace!"

After we lost my father we heard the most wonderful singing in the hush of the hour before twilight; and we could hardly believe that the rapturous melody which thrilled our souls and seemed to bring heaven quite near to us could come from the throat of a bird.

Another strange thing happened after the tombstone had been placed over my father's grave. One day my mother noticed that a tiny plant was growing between the crevices in the ground, and she allowed it to remain. Gradually this plant became a flowering tree, with rich clusters of bloom. There it blossomed season after season; but when my mother's gravestone was being placed, the tree was cut down by a mistake of the masons, and it never grew again. I often think of that wonderful growth. It seemed like a bright message of hope from him whose departure had cast so deep a shadow on all our lives.

Chapter VII

LIFE AT COOCH BEHAR

Eight days after I lost my father I held a little daughter in my arms, and I wondered whether the innocent soul which had come into my keeping straight from God had met my father's noble spirit on its upward flight.

Into that house of mourning her birth brought some consolation. We named her Sukriti (Good deeds), but we always call her Girlie. She is fascinating rather than lovely.

When Rajey was four years old, as no other son had been born to us, the Maharajah's people were most anxious for him to marry again, for they said if anything happened to the child and the Maharajah also died, the throne would have to go to another branch of the family. The old Maharani and the late Calica Das Duth planned out very carefully that it was most necessary for my husband to marry again. The Maharajah never mentioned the matter to me, but to the doctor he said when Rajey once had an attack of false croup: "Durga Das, I shall always be over-anxious about Rajey's health until another son is born." So it was a day of great rejoicing when my second son Jitendra, whom we called Jit, was born, 20th December, 1886.

I was greatly delighted when I went to live at Cooch Behar to find there a fine church of the New Dispensation and a girls' school named after me.

But there was much room for improvement in the country, although Government had well prepared the way for us. It remained for my husband to be a ruler in the highest sense of the word, and for me to win the hearts of our people as a woman, a wife, and a mother. The more I saw of Cooch Behar the more I liked it. The old tales say that the god Siva chose it as his earthly home on account of its luxuriant loveliness.

Many legends have gathered round Cooch Behar, mostly of the time when it formed part of the kingdom of Kamrupa, and when many of the temples and palaces were built.

Among the stories is that of a Maharajah of Cooch Behar who had a number of wives, one of whom was a very pretty girl; she was the favourite wife and the others were very jealous of her. The Prime Minister had a very handsome son, who when walking one day in the palace gardens, looked up and caught sight of her beautiful eyes looking out of a window of the palace. He gazed at the lovely face, and the girl, who had never seen any man except her husband, stared back at him. The young man thought he had never seen any one so beautiful, and in the days that followed he often came to the garden. Unfortunately, some of the ladies of the palace saw him looking at the little Maharani in the window. It did not take long for the Maharajah to learn this, and he promised the wife who told him a handsome present if she had spoken the truth.

One day when the romantic pair were thus engaged in gazing at each other from a distance, the Maharajah saw them. Naturally, though unjustly, he suspected his wife's fidelity. He sent a message to the Prime Minister commanding him to dine at the palace that evening. The Dewan, as he believed, greatly honoured, accepted the invitation.

After dinner the Maharajah said: "I have a present for you to take home." When he reached his house, the Prime Minister told his wife to open the parcel. Directly afterwards he heard a terrible scream, and, rushing into his wife's room, found her on the floor unconscious, with a half-open parcel which contained the head of his son. The Dewan guessed at once what had happened. Without a word he left his house just as he was, and started for Delhi, the capital of the Moghul Empire. Arrived there, he begged an audience, and when admitted to the presence of the Emperor he told him that Cooch Behar was one of the richest districts in India and suggested he should try to conquer it. The Emperor made several attacks on Cooch Behar; but the fort was so strong that each time his army was driven back from the place now known as Moghulhat.

This story is only one of the many I have heard. Their trend is always the same. The members of my husband's ancient race have been brave soldiers, generous alike to friend and foe, and passionate lovers, and they have sought afar for their wives.

I have often thought how uncharitable the general public are about the failings of those in high places. Without knowing them well, without knowing their inner lives, the public have an unjust habit of writing and speaking unkindly of rulers and princes. Often the public will compare their own lives with the lives of their princes— a commoner's with a ruler's life! God has chosen one man to be a ruler and others to be his subjects. It is unfair to judge hastily without knowing the divine object of each life; people who rashly judge often do grave injustice to those who have been called to a high station.

When I first came to Cooch Behar we lived in the old palace, which was like a town. Hundreds of ladies occupied the various houses of which it was composed: the late Maharajah's wives, his mother and grandmother, and many relations, with all their servants. Whenever there were festivities all these ladies gathered together and it was like a great crowd in a small city.

Now we live in the new palace, which is considered one of the finest in India. It was designed by a Western architect and is built in an eclectic style. It boasts a fine Durbar Hall, and the east front consists of a range of arcades along the ground and narrow piers, and the cement and terra-cotta used in the construction make an effective decoration. On one side of the palace is the swimming bath, and covered racket and tennis courts. The gardens are lovely. There is a river on the west, a town towards the east, and to the north in the far distance stand the great Himalayas like a fort. In the winter months on clear days we can see the snow distinctly. In the spring, flowers bloom everywhere, and as for fireflies, although I have travelled far, I have never seen so many thousands together; on dark nights they look like little stars twinkling in the fields. During the rains all the rivers, of which there are many, are in flood, and then I think of Cooch Behar as something like Venice. The thunderstorms at times are terrific; our old nurse, Mrs. Eldridge, used to say: "In all my travels I have never experienced such thunderstorms." We had English nurses for all our children, except Rajey. I was highly amused at Mrs. Eldridge's surprise when she first came. I asked her why she appeared to be so interested in me, and received this blunt reply: "Well, your Highness, when I came to take up my duties with you, I expected to find a stout, dark, uneducated lady. I must say, now that I've seen you, I'm so taken aback that I can hardly believe my eyes."

My day was always much occupied. After my morning tea, the children often brought me flowers from the garden and I used to make sketches of them, and this was the pleasure and pride of my life. After my bath I put on a silk sari, which is supposed to be sacred, and arranged the prayer-room. I loved the effect of the masses of roses, jessamine, and the bright-hued flowers against the white marble of the altar and floor. The open windows admitted the sweet air, fresh from the river close by.

I prepared the fruits and sweets for the household, and have often prepared enough vegetables for fifty people. My readers may perhaps smile at the idea of a Maharani cutting vegetables! I used to sit on the floor surrounded by the brass bowls in which the vegetables were washed, and the maids constantly changed the water for me. I always cut enough vegetables to fill several large plates, for we generally had eighteen curries for each meal. I also used to slice betel-nut, which has to be cut very fine, and sometimes filled several big jars at one time. Often I made sweets, as both my husband and the children were fond of sweets. I also prepared pickles of mangoes, and potatoes, and other vegetables; all this I had learned to do from my dear mother.

Sometimes I used to make up betel leaves into tiny odd-shaped packets filled with half a dozen different spices, and pinned together with cloves. Perhaps most English readers do not know what a valuable digestive the betel leaf is. It strengthens the gums, and completely neutralises the bad effects of indigestible delicacies.

Sometimes the Maharajah came in while I was cutting the vegetables, and he would sit and watch me, occasionally saying: "Take care, you'll cut yourself," just as though I were a little girl who did not know how to peel a potato. Now and again I would get up tableaux and plays to amuse my relations-in-law, the officers' wives, and others, and these they seemed to enjoy greatly. I was very fond of painting, and often spent hours ornamenting the mantelpieces and the glass panes in the doors. We made a miniature garden which the children loved. In this garden we had a tank filled with clear water, in which one day my second son, the present Maharajah, then a little boy, wanted to have a bath. We tried to dissuade him, but he insisted on having his own way, so we undressed him and put him in the tank. He felt the cold but pretended he was quite warm, and he looked like a picture with only his face and curly head showing above the water in the little tank surrounded by flowers.

From the day of his accession to the throne the Maharajah devoted all the earnestness of his nature and his great powers of organisation to plans for the comfort, well-being, and education of his subjects. New roads were made; the systematic development of the resources of the State was undertaken, and hospitals, schools, and public buildings were erected. Some of these are very fine; the Masonic Lodge in Cooch Behar is one of the largest in Bengal. The Maharajah took a keen interest in questions of education and founded a college of which he was very proud. At a distribution of prizes at this college on one occasion he said: "If I find any boys guilty of disloyalty they shall be turned out of the State in twenty-four hours."

Hindu princes are allowed to marry as many wives as they wish, but the Maharanis are part of the State, and there is a vast difference between their position and that of the other palace ladies. The ruler's wives are brought to the palace as little girls, there to be married and afterwards educated, solely, I am obliged to admit, with the idea of attracting their husband, who, more often than not, never sees half of them. Nevertheless the pretty ones learn to sing, dance, and cook to perfection, for in many palaces the Maharajah's food is never touched by paid cooks. Some keep accounts. All are busy with their work and, my mother-in-law told me, they are quite happy. Some of my readers may have heard that any girl may become a Rajah's wife. This is absolutely untrue; the Maharanis must be young girls of good family, and always are. The Rajah's wives are not allowed to go out to other houses. It may be my weakness or my strength, but I have altered my position in this respect a little; I do see people if urged, but I have often been asked by my husband's relations to remember who I am, and not to speak to any and everybody, and lower my position.

My mother-in-law was a well-built woman, rather short but wonderfully strong. She was bright and always full of fun. Her kind help made my life a happy one, and her wise counsel often guided me in hours of difficulty when I first went to Cooch Behar, after my marriage. She died of cholera at Woodlands; Rajey, a cousin of mine, and I nursed her through her last illness.

The Maharajah had a step-brother and sister, both very handsome; they were very devoted to my dear husband, especially the sister.

There is a custom in the palace that no one shall have a meal before the Maharajah. For a few years I kept up this custom strictly; but sometimes, when I was in indifferent health, I found it difficult to wait until one or two o'clock in the afternoon for my breakfast. The Maharajah came to know of this and asked me why I did not have my breakfast earlier. When he heard of the custom he said to his mother, "The Maharani cannot possibly wait so long. She is to have her meals before me, if I am delayed." His mother did not like this at all, but as it was a command she had to obey.

We do not have many meals in India. Formerly we had breakfast, fruit and milk every afternoon, and dinner. Now we have quite a late breakfast in the English way, and afternoon tea. Until I left India I had never tasted meat. Our delicious fruits would convert the most ardent meat-lover into a fruitarian.

How I love Cooch Behar with its abundance of birds and flowers! The scenery is glorious, the beautiful lotus covers the rivers, and at some of the old religious festivals the temples are lavishly decorated with the gorgeous pink blossoms. The Cooch Behar climate is splendid; the winters are like those of the South of France, and the spring is heavenly.

I endeavoured from the first to gain the confidence and affection of my husband's subjects, and I never knowingly ran counter to their prejudices. In Darjeeling and Calcutta I may be considered the Maharani with advanced Western ideas, but in Cooch Behar I was and am the zenana lady who enters into the lives of the people. Many who at first looked upon my marriage with disfavour took me to their hearts when they found that I was just like all their Maharanis, and that I loved them.

Now when I feel that earthly happiness and myself have parted company, I like to picture Rajey as he was in those days. He had large sad eyes, lovely curling hair, and he grew into a straight-limbed slender boy, beautiful as the legendary sons of Siva.

In January, 1884, soon after we lost my father, we went to Simla. There Rajey sickened with typhoid fever and became seriously ill, and the doctors in attendance declared the case to be hopeless. My husband's distress was terrible, and I shall never forget his anguished words: "If God will only spare Rajey's life, Sunity, you and I would give our lives for him."

Our prayers were answered. After six weeks' fight with death our child was restored to us. Rajey's nature was always sweetly unselfish, even as a little boy. When I used to tell him stories the sad parts always made him cry.

"How do rulers get their money?" he asked me one day.

"Well, Rajey, by taxing people."

"Shall I be a ruler?"

"Yes, darling, I hope you will some day."

"Then," he announced, his great eyes shining, "I'll never ask for any taxes until everybody is well off and quite able to pay."

Once I met him laden with all his boots and shoes. "Rajey, where are you going?" I asked. I was told that one of his servants had informed the boy that he was too poor to buy shoes for his children, and the kind little Rajey had straightway started off to remedy the trouble.

Rajey was loyal to a degree. His creed was "once a friend, always a friend." He never went back after he had extended the hand of friendship to any one. In later years he was often deceived by those he trusted and belittled by those who had received innumerable kindnesses from him, but I never once heard him speak unkindly.

His loyalty forbade it, and although he must have been wounded, he suffered in silence.

I remember another incident of those early days; Rajey was hit by his bearer, an act which made every one indignant and was immediately reported to me. My husband, who never permitted any one to touch the children, told one of the officers to question the bearer, and the man flatly denied having laid a finger on Rajey.

"I know the boy never tells a lie," remarked the Maharajah; "send for Rajey and I will ask him."

The child came in, and my husband said quietly: "Now were you beaten?" No answer. "Rajey, tell me the truth, there's a dear boy." Still no answer. "Rajey … do you hear me speaking?" Again no reply. "Well, then," said my husband, "go and stand in the corner until you tell me if the bearer hit you."

Rajey obeyed and occupied the corner, the tears rolling down his cheeks, but he refused to tell about the offender, and I believe my husband loved the boy all the more because of his loyal but misplaced affection for his servant.

On another occasion when our English secretary's boys were fighting, and the younger was getting the worst of the struggle, Rajey cried: "Stop! it's not fair; nobody ought to hit a boy smaller than himself."

He had a strong sense of justice and his father was his ideal. Whatever my husband did was right in the eyes of his first-born. No one was so wonderful nor so good as his father. Our doctor once said: "Rajey, I'm taller than your father." "You dare say that," the child answered in furious tones; "nobody in the world can possibly be taller than my father."

Rajey was, even when a small boy, impressed with a sense of the responsibilities of those whose destiny it is to govern others. He seemed to realise the hollowness of earthly state, and he never tired of listening to one of our stories which, like most Indian legends, has a striking moral. Its simple cynicism may interest my readers.

Once the souls of the poor were standing in front of the closed gates of heaven. Since they parted from their bodies they had patiently spent many weary days hoping for admittance to the lovely country where the ills of life are forgotten. The horrors of their past lives had not yet faded from their minds, although in this place of waiting they were spared the pangs of poverty, hunger, and thirst.

The vast multitude gazed yearningly at the gates which did not open. Suddenly word came, "Make way, make way, O souls, a rich Maharajah's spirit is on its way to heaven and must be instantly admitted."

The poor murmured together, but again the gatekeeper spoke, and the crowd parted to give place to the soul of the Maharajah.

At last it came. And the poor caught a glimpse of the pomp and circumstance which attended its passage to heaven. The gates were flung open, the perfumed air of Paradise came forth for an instant, but the poor remained outside.

"Ah!" cried the weary spirits. "Is existence still to be the same for us as it was when we lived upon earth? There the rich always oppressed us. We were as dust under their feet. We toiled that they might have the luxuries they demanded. And now that we are dead we still suffer. Why should we not be admitted to heaven without delay? Alas! there is no justice at the hands of God since the soul of a Maharajah but lately dead takes precedence of us."

"Oh, silence, rebellious ones!" cried the gatekeeper. "Surely, surely, you know that the road to heaven is an easy one for the poor to traverse. You have no temptations in your passage save the ills of poverty. You have not to combat with the lust of the eye, with the arrogance of riches, with the evil wrought by flattering tongues and the misuse of power. Think what allurements this ruler must have resisted in order to prepare himself for heaven. It is a stupendous feat for a Maharajah to have accomplished, and," added the gatekeeper unctuously, "we seldom see them here, therefore it behoves me to give instant admittance to such a rare arrival."

And the souls of the poor were silent, for they recognised the words of wisdom which the gatekeeper had spoken.

Chapter VIII

MY FIRST VISIT TO ENGLAND

The year 1887 was expected to be a memorable one for India, as our late beloved Queen-Empress would celebrate her Jubilee. India was anxious to show her loyalty to the Sovereign whose high ideals and humanity have endeared her to all her people. Many of our princes therefore decided to render their homage in person. My husband made his plans for this eventful year long beforehand, but he cleverly kept all of us in the dark as to his intention that I should accompany him to England. It must be remembered that the conditions of life among Indian ladies were very different in 1887 from what they are to-day. The Maharani of Baroda, I believe, had once gone to Switzerland, but for the wife of a ruler to visit England with her husband caused quite a sensation. I think I am right in saying that I was the first Maharani to do such a thing, and I may as well confess that I dreaded the experience. I knew absolutely nothing about the journey. I was going to be a stranger in a strange land, and I was sensitive enough to dread being stared at, for I well knew that this must be my fate in London. We sailed on the P. and O. boat Ganges or Ballarat, I forget which. I remember the captain of the boat took great pains to ensure our comfort on board. Our suite consisted of my two brothers Nirmul and Profulla, two A.D.C.'s, J. Raikut and S. Sing, our English private secretary, the late Mr. Bignell and his family, and our English nurse, besides our two selves and our three little children. We also had some Indian servants. I cannot describe my feelings when I realised that I had actually left India, had passed another milestone on life's road, but I little dreamed that the far-off country for which I was bound was destined to be a land of sorrow for me in the distant future. The glory of the sea enchanted me. When the boat was out on the ocean and no land could be seen, all Nature seemed to speak of the infinite God, and I felt so small. In the dark evenings when the water gleamed with phosphorescence, it looked as if there were thousands of stars under the sea responding to the stars above. It really was grand; a grandeur that no one could describe unless he had actually experienced it. Before we embarked I had tasted meat for the first time in my life, and I disliked the flavour so much that for the first few days of the voyage I ate nothing but a few vegetables. I often had fits of depression and sometimes left the dinner table to relieve my feelings with a good cry.

The Maharajah parted from us at Port Said, as it was decided that it would be easier and less fatiguing for me with my little ones to go by sea instead of taking the shorter route across Europe. I was delighted when I first saw Malta and Gibraltar. Mr. Bignell met us at Tilbury Docks. Just as we were seated in the train, I was handed a message from Queen Victoria that she wished to see me at Court in my national dress. It was May, but very cold for the time of year, and my first sight of London on a Sunday did not raise my spirits. I saw half-deserted streets swept with a bitter wind which had already chapped my face, and I was heartily glad when at last we reached the Grosvenor Hotel. There all was brightness and animation. My husband was so pleased to see me and the children and to show me the grand suite of rooms which had been reserved for us. The housekeeper at the Grosvenor had thought of everything that would make us comfortable, and my memory of her is of a pleasant woman with plenty of common sense. One thing I did not like. Our luxurious suite of rooms had no bathroom. I was told I was to have a bath in my room, but this I would not do. I was shown to a big bath, but was horrified when I was told that I must pass all those corridors each time I wanted a bath. I refused point-blank, and they finally prepared a small room as a bathroom for me.

Kind invitations poured in, and I was happy to see many old friends. I shall never forget the question Sir Ashley Eden put to me: "What do you think of our London fog?" for although it was May, I had experienced a yellow fog. I answered: "Not much, Sir Ashley; I do not think I shall ever care for the London fog." We dined at Sir Ashley's, and there I first met the present Lord Crewe. We had a large drawing-room at the hotel which I could never make cosy or comfortable; on rainy days especially, it felt damp and gloomy. When I went out for drives I used to see little children with their toy boats in Hyde Park, and I soon got a nice little sailing yacht for my Rajey, and both mother and son enjoyed floating this vessel on the Serpentine. Rajey's little face beamed with delight when he saw his boat going along. The late Lady Rosebery was most kind to my little ones; Rajey and Girlie spent some happy afternoons at her house. The present Lady Crewe was a small girl then, and her brother, Lord Dalmeny, made a great friend of dear Rajey and always remained the same.

Soon after we arrived in London I was alarmed to find my baby Jit develop bronchitis. Both my husband and I were most anxious about the child, and their own doctors were offered by two Royal ladies, one of whom was H.R.H. the Princess of Wales, now Queen

Alexandra. When Jit got better the nursery was often honoured by
two Royal visitors, H.R.H. the late Duchess of Teck and our present
Queen, then Princess May. These two charming ladies graciously
came and played with my children. It was lovely to see little Jit in
Princess May's arms. I have seldom met so sweet a personality as
the Duchess of Teck. She simply radiated kindness and good nature.
One glance at her happy, handsome face inspired confidence. I was
greatly honoured when she said she would chaperone me during the
Jubilee festivities. The present Queen was then a tall graceful girl,
with a wild-rose freshness and fairness, and gifted with the same
simple unaffected charm of manner as her mother, which had
already endeared her to me.

It had been intimated to me that Queen Victoria wished to see me
privately before the Court, and it was arranged that I should go to
Buckingham Palace for an audience. The question of what I was to
wear had to be settled. The Maharajah, who always displayed the
greatest interest in my toilets, chose and ordered my gown for this
great occasion. I was extremely nervous, and as I saw my reflection
in the mirror in the pale grey dress I felt more terrified than ever.
My maid, seeing me look so pale and shaken, brought me a glass of
port. I never touch wine, except when it is absolutely necessary. My
hand trembled so that I spilt half of the wine over my gown.
Instantly a chorus of "How lucky" arose. But I gazed rather ruefully
at the stains.

"Well, Sunity, it is time for us to start," said my husband, and I
followed him to the carriage. Lord Cross, who was then Secretary
of State for India, received us, and his wife whispered a few

reassuring words to me before the officials escorted us down the corridors to the small room where Her Majesty was.

I cannot describe my feelings when I found myself in the presence of the Queen. To us Indians she was a more or less legendary figure endowed with wonderful attributes, an ideal ruler, and an ideal woman, linked to our hearts across "the black water" by silken chains of love and loyalty. I looked at Her Majesty anxiously, and my first impression instantly dispelled my nervousness: a short, stout lady dressed in mourning who came forward and kissed me twice. I made a deep curtsy, and walked a step backward, and then my husband came forward and bent low over the Queen's hand. I experienced a feeling, as did every one with whom Her late Majesty came in contact, that she possessed great personal magnetism, and she certainly was the embodiment of dignity. Her conversation was simple and kindly, and every word revealed her queen, woman and mother. I was delighted to find that I had not been disappointed in my ideal, and felt eager to go back to India that I might tell my country-women about our wonderful Empress. The audience occupied only a few minutes, but nothing could have exceeded Her Majesty's graciousness, and I came away proud and glad, and laughed at myself for my previous terror at being received by one so gracious. The Maharajah was very pleased at our reception, and told me how proud he was of me.

The next day we attended the Drawing-room. I wore a white and gold brocade gown and a crêpe de Chine sari. I waited with the other ladies, and as it was a cold afternoon I was very glad to find a little cosy corner and sit down. I looked around me, and was admiring the pretty dresses and faces when I suddenly saw what I thought was a gentleman wearing a diamond tiara. I gazed at the face and then discovered it belonged to a lady who had a thick moustache. I went into the throne-room, and as I was told by Lady Cross that I need not kiss Her Majesty when I made my curtsy, as I had already been received privately, when Her Majesty wanted to kiss me I avoided her! After finishing my curtsies I went on to the next and the next, and I distinctly heard the Queen say to the Princess of Wales: "Why would not the Maharani kiss me?" This made me so nervous that I thought I should drop on the floor. After I had finished making all my curtsies I went and stood near kind Lady Salisbury and watched the other ladies pass. One of the duchesses, an elderly woman in a very low dress trimmed with old lace and wearing magnificent jewels, to my mind looked extremely miserable. I can still see her trembling as she curtsied; whether it was the cold or her aged body was tired I cannot say. I was greatly interested in all I saw; but shocked at the low-cut gowns worn by the ladies present. The cold was most trying to complexions and shoulders, the prevailing tints of which were either brick-red or a chilly reddish-blue. Now that the Courts are held in the evenings women's beauty is seen to greater advantage, but I shall never forget that May afternoon and the inartistic exposure of necks and arms.

We received an invitation for the State ball. My husband chose a gown of blue and silver brocade for me for this important occasion. Just before we left the hotel for the palace the Maharajah said: "Sunity, if the Prince of Wales asks you to dance with him, you must; it would be a very great honour." "I can't," I faltered, "I simply can't; you know I do not dance." "Never mind, you cannot refuse your future king." "Well," I said, "I don't think I will go; let me send a letter of apology." "Impossible! We are bound to attend; it is a command." I said no more, but prayed and hoped that I might be overlooked by the Prince. Not so, however. Soon after we entered the ballroom a message was sent by H.R.H. asking me to dance with him. I returned the answer that, although I greatly appreciated the honour, I must refuse as I never danced. Then came another message: It was only the Lancers, and H.R.H. would show me the steps.

Again I refused; then, to my great surprise, the late King George of Greece came up to where I was sitting. "Do come and dance, Maharani," he said, "I assure you there is nothing in it."

"Please forgive me, your Majesty," I stammered, "but I cannot dance." The late King of Denmark, then Crown Prince, also graciously asked me to dance. By this time I was too nervous for words, and I heard a sweet voice say: "Oh, look! hasn't the Maharani tiny little feet?" I glanced in an agony of shyness at the dais from whence the tones proceeded, quite close to where I was sitting, and saw that the speaker was none other than the Princess of Wales! I did not know what to do, and felt for the moment as if I were all feet. My skirt was rather short, and I could not tuck my shoes out of sight. I was very glad and relieved when suppertime came. I went in with the Royal Family to supper. Every one was most gracious, and the Prince of Wales teased me about my not accepting him as a partner.

"What do you think of the ball?" asked one of the Princesses. "It is a grand sight, Ma'am; I think the jewels are wonderful." I was introduced to several foreign royalties, and one girl I loved directly

I saw her. She was the Grand Duchess Sergius of Russia, with whom I afterwards became very friendly.

On the morning of the Jubilee I was early astir. I wore a pale orange-coloured gown with a sari to match. We left the hotel at a quarter-past nine. As we drove to the Abbey I was struck with the perfect behaviour of the crowd.

It was a hot, dusty drive, and I was glad of the shade of my parasol. Suddenly a shout arose. "Put down that sunshade, please, and let's have a look at you."

"Don't," whispered the Maharajah, "you'll get sunstroke." I hesitated. "Come now, put it down." I closed my parasol, and as I did so was heartily cheered. "That's right," roared the good-humoured crowd, "thank you very much."

On entering the Abbey we were escorted to our seats.

It was an impressive ceremony, and the Queen looked inspired when she came back from the altar. After the service was over, as Her Majesty walked down the aisle, her eyes met mine, and she smiled. I was the only Maharani present, and I like to remember this signal honour.

A striking figure in that vast assembly was the late Emperor Frederick of Germany, who was a very handsome man. His appearance was so noble it was a delight to watch his looks and dignity. There was a grand but rather small evening party at Buckingham Palace on the same day as the Jubilee ceremony at Westminster. Her Majesty, looking very happy, stood in the middle of the room, with all the foreign Princes and Princesses in their full-dress costumes, and covered with splendid jewels and decorations, around her. After making my curtsies to Her Majesty and the Royal

Princesses, I was introduced to several foreign Royalties, one of whom was the late Grand Duke of Hesse. I shall never forget the charming way in which the Duchess of Connaught presented him to me; she just said: "My brother-in-law, the Grand Duke." I don't think the world has ever witnessed such a wonderful Royal gathering as that, with such magnificent jewels, and full-dress uniforms of brilliant colours, and the array of medals and orders that covered many breasts. One and all looked happy, and that in itself made the party a "great success." Our congratulations to Her Majesty on her Jubilee were sincere, loyal, and warm.

Life passed very swiftly and pleasantly for me during the Jubilee celebrations, and I was thoroughly spoiled, much to the delight of my husband. I have many recollections of that memorable year, and can picture to myself many of my kind and charming hostesses. I remember once in the supper-room at Buckingham Palace my husband introduced the Ex-Kaiser, then Prince William, to me, and the young prince bent down and kissed my hand. I blushed and my throat grew dry; my hand had never been kissed before by a man. After the Prince left us I tried to scold my husband in Bengali, but he laughed, and said: "Sunity, it is a great honour that your hand should be kissed by the future German Emperor; you ought to feel proud." I admired Prince William and the way in which the foreign Royalties showed their respect for ladies.

We went to Windsor Castle one day to present our gifts to Her Majesty. My husband chose a little diamond pendant with an uncut ruby in the middle, and told me to give it to Her Majesty. I said to my husband: "I shall be too nervous," but he urged me: "Just a few words, Sunity; it will please Her Majesty." Little did my husband know what those few words cost me. We went by special train to Windsor, and when we arrived at the Castle we were received by the equerries and high officials. It was the day for Indians to pay their homage to their Empress. Captain Muir was in command of the bodyguard on duty. We entered the throne-room where the Queen was, and I presented our little present with a few words to Her Majesty, who graciously accepted it and thanked me. I made a deep curtsy and walked backwards, feeling nervous at the thought of mistakes in my little speech and curtsy, but people who were present in the room said afterwards the Maharani of Cooch Behar's words were clear and her curtsy was most graceful.

One evening we dined with Mr. and Miss Kinnaird. The table was decorated with masses of scarlet roses specially sent over from Paris. The perfume of the roses took my memory back to the old Belghuria garden. I enjoyed this dinner very much. We were going on to an evening party at the Guildhall, and the Maharajah asked one of the gentlemen in the Royal suite who was at the dinner whether full dress or evening dress was expected. "Ordinary evening dress, your Highness," was the reply. However, to our dismay, when we reached the Guildhall we found all the men were in full dress. My husband felt very uncomfortable at being the only man in evening dress, and would not go near the Royal dais; a fact which did not escape the notice of the Prince of Wales. His Royal Highness sent for my husband. "What's the matter, Maharajah?" he inquired, and the reason was explained. The Prince was anxious to know the name of the gentleman who had made the mistake, but my husband would not give him away. Thereupon the Prince turned to me and said with a smile: "Oh, Maharani, you are a very careless wife. You haven't dressed your husband properly." Every one smiled, and the Prince's kindly tact put the Maharajah completely at his ease. When we went into the supper-room, Her Majesty the late Empress Frederick came and stood beside me and asked many questions about Indian home-life and customs. Her Majesty said: "How do you address your husband? Do you call him by his name?" I said: "No, Ma'am, we generally address our husbands in the third person." "How would you call your husband if you wanted him now?" I said: "Ogo." "What does that mean?" asked the Empress. "Please, dear." She laughed, and they all, the Empress included, began to call each other "Ogo." Then Her Majesty looked at my hair and asked: "Is that all your own hair?" "Yes, Ma'am," I said. "What a lovely lot of hair you have!"

I admired everybody and everything with whole-hearted admiration, but I think my utmost meed of devotion was paid to Queen Alexandra (then Princess of Wales), who was as kind as she was beautiful, and so womanly that my heart went out to her.

I first discovered at a dinner given by a bachelor friend of the Maharajah's that punctuality was not considered a virtue in London. The invitation was for 7.45, but the last guest did not arrive until ten minutes to nine, and I was told that "no one is ever punctual in London." I was so tired that I fainted with the arrival of the soup, but revived enough to eat dinner, and we afterwards went on to an entertainment where I saw Letty Lind dance. She was then a pretty girl and danced exquisitely. To our great pleasure and pride the Prince of Wales came and sat in our box. My husband said to me in Bengali: "Do ask His Royal Highness if he will honour us with his company at supper," and when I did ask, how graciously he accepted and thanked us! We knew he had a party of his own, and I could not help thinking: "It must be because H.R.H. is fond of my husband that he did not refuse," and I appreciated the honour all the more. As the Prince left our dining-room, one of the gentlemen of our party overheard him remark to his equerry: "I do like Cooch Behar, he is such a straightforward man." I remember how pleased I was when these words were repeated to me. That was my husband all through his life—straightforward. He scorned the subterfuges which those of his rank often adopt to please a censorious world. He was outspoken, and one who was never ashamed of his friends, whatever their position might be. Although he was the proudest of men, his simplicity was such that he believed his joie de vivre would pass unnoticed, and that he might sometimes be allowed to live as a man and not as a Maharajah.

Queen Victoria displayed the most kindly interest in our doings. One day I was invited to take the children to Windsor Castle. I dressed them in their national costume, which pleased Her Majesty exceedingly. After a few minutes' conversation the Queen said to me: "Do you remember this pendant, Maharani?"

I looked and saw that she was wearing the jewel which we had had the honour of presenting to Her Majesty. I felt very touched at the thought of her wearing our gift, and told Her Majesty so.

When we were saying good-bye the Queen graciously said: "You must let the children have some strawberries and fruit which I have had prepared in another room." The children were not shy, and I never saw strawberries disappear so fast. Rajey soon confined his attention to some magnificent hothouse grapes. "Come away," I said, for I began to dread the result of a prolonged riot in fruit. Both obeyed; but Rajey lifted up two enormous bunches of grapes and carried them off, much to the delight of Her Majesty.

I remember, too, how the late Emperor Frederick admired our little Jit, and taking the boy's hand in his, said many kind words to him. I also had the great pleasure of seeing the Empress of Russia, then Princess Alex of Hesse, a young girl of sixteen, sitting on the carpet in the corridor playing with some small children and dogs. Her thick plait was hanging down her back, and when she lifted her large dark eyes, I said to myself: "What a lovely face and what sad eyes!" It was indeed good to live in those happy days. What a pleasant picture I have in my memory of that afternoon of sunshine, friendly faces, and the Queen and Princess Beatrice waving us farewell!

I was once invited by the late Duchess of Connaught to lunch with H.R.H. at Windsor Castle. Mrs. Bignell accompanied me. It was indeed a great honour, as the Duchess did not ask any one but me. I was touched to find a King's daughter, a Queen's daughter-in-law, living like a very ordinary mother in her own home. I would have given much for my country-women to have seen the Duchess that day, with her little children.

We went to a grand garden-party at Buckingham Palace, at which thousands of men and women were assembled; it was a striking sight. I don't think any one ever got a better chance of seeing so many pretty faces together. We were all waiting for the Queen's arrival when some people came and asked us to make a passage for Her Majesty to pass. My husband stood right at the back, but I was always anxious to see everything, and stood in the front line. To my surprise Her Majesty walked straight up to me and kissed me, and I believe I was the only woman there whom the Queen kissed. I was greatly amused the following day when the newspapers made some sarcastic remarks about the Indian Princess receiving more attention than any of the others.

Another day we were commanded to dine with Her Majesty at Windsor Castle and spend the night there. When the train stopped at Windsor station we found a red carpet on the platform and the Royal carriage in waiting. Officers came to receive us; I felt quite grand, and how the crowd cheered us, and many a kind remark I heard from them. We drove up to the castle, and when we arrived we went straight to our rooms. I never saw anything so splendid and yet so comfortable. The sitting-room was facing the park, which was lovely in the sunshine, and the bedroom was all gilt from ceiling to floor—it was like fairyland. The only thing that puzzled me was that there should be no bathroom to such a lavishly furnished suite. I asked my husband in despair: "Can't I have a bath after such a journey?" The Maharajah in his calm, quiet way said: "Sunity, there must be a bath in this room," and he began to look for a door. Suddenly he found a button-like knob, and on pressing it a door sprang open, and there was a large room and a bath; I screamed with joy at the sight. I was struck with another thing; the face towels were of the finest linen. We had tea, and the Maharajah told me that if I received a present from Her Majesty I must thank her nicely. I kept on asking him what the present was, and why I should have it. My husband did not answer, and so I left off worrying him. I had not quite finished dressing when the Maharajah came and said an officer had come to show us where we were to wait for Her Majesty. This made me more nervous than ever, and I could not put on my jewels properly, so my husband helped me to carry some necklets, bracelets, a fan, and gloves. As we came into the ante-room I was relieved to find that we were the first to arrive and I had time to put on the jewels and gloves. Her Royal Highness Princess Beatrice entered first, and soon alter Her Majesty walked in with a jewel-case in her hand. She gave it to me and kissed me and I curtsied several times, thanking Her Majesty for the gift. It was the decoration C.I., "Crown of India." Her Majesty said a few words with it which I appreciated even more than the present. Her Majesty asked the Princess to pin it on for me, which H.R.H. did. I was no longer nervous, as both the Princess and Her Majesty were most gracious and kind and made me feel quite happy. Prince Henry of Battenberg was a dark, handsome man and seemed very nice. After a few minutes' talk we walked into the dining-room. This was not a big room, but Her Majesty's own private room. There were portraits of the Queen's three daughters-in-law; that of the Princess of Wales as a bride was exquisite. Her Majesty sat in the middle, my husband on her right, Princess Beatrice on her left, and then me. When champagne went round and I refused it, Her Majesty noticed and asked my husband the reason. The Maharajah said I never took champagne or wine. This did not annoy the good Queen, but seemed to please her. Her Majesty and Princess Beatrice both very kindly asked after my dear mother and grandmother, and how well Her Majesty remembered my revered father; she had a photograph of him. While we were at dinner we heard another guest had arrived, but he would not have any English food. After dinner was over this guest came in to see Her Majesty. He was an Indian Maharajah. We talked for some time after dinner. Princess Beatrice asked why more of our Indian ladies did not come to England, as H.M. the Queen loved seeing them. We stayed the night, but I do not think I slept much; lying in the gold bed I almost fancied myself a fairy princess. This suite of rooms was the Princess of Wales's, so it was a great honour for us to have them.

There was no marked ceremony at these Royal parties, and everything was delightfully informal. There stand out in my memory a luncheon at Marlborough House, when the Princess of Wales gave me a lovely Russian cypher brooch, and a tête-à-tête tea with her on another occasion when I took my babies with me. Jit was tremendously attracted by our beautiful hostess, who took his hand, saying as she did so: "What a pretty little boy! no wonder his mother was so anxious when he was ill."

The kindness shown me by Queen Alexandra has never varied since those early days. Fate has dealt heavily with us both. We have each lost our idolised first-born. We have each lost the best of husbands. We have equally sorrowed. I think some subtle sympathy draws us together; each time I have visited her of late I have been struck afresh by her resigned expression, and I know that the Queen-Mother feels as I do, that "There's not a joy the world can give like those it takes away."

Chapter IX

ENGLISH SOCIETY

The Princess of Wales asked me one day what I thought of the shops in Bond Street, and if I often went to them. But somehow I never went into any except my dressmaker, Madame Oliver Holmes's, and Hamley's toy shop, where I felt like buying the whole shop, or spending all my time, it charmed me so much.

I enjoyed the theatres. One of the plays I shall ever remember was Shakespeare's "Winter's Tale." Mary Anderson acted in it; it was magnificently staged, and Mary Anderson's lovely face and good acting impressed me. One opera I went to—I forget the name—reminded me of our Indian love story, "Nal and Damayanti," as swans come and bring love messages from lovers apart. Her Majesty had graciously lent us her box, and I think Madame Albani sang. I was much interested in the British Museum, and could have spent days and days looking at all the wonderful things in it. At the Naval Review I went to see the boats decorated with lights—the reflections in the water were splendid. I also went to see the Royal stable, a visit arranged for me by the late Lord Elphinstone, and Rajey was put in the Royal coach. I went to see Madame Tussaud's, and was delighted with the figures, but had not the courage to go down into the Chamber of Horrors. I was much impressed by a large picture of the late Prince Imperial with the Zulus attacking him. I went to see the Tower of London and was much interested. We also visited Edinburgh: what a lovely town it is! We went to the castle, and my childhood came back to me as my eldest brother had told me the story of this castle when we were children. We went to Holyrood Palace one afternoon. The guide as usual began to show me every room and every corner of the palace relating all the stories attached, which took hours, and the Maharajah grew tired, as I kept him with me, telling him every time he wanted to go: "I won't be long." But when the guide brought some bits of the old paper from the walls in Queen Mary's time the Maharajah got quite impatient. It rained and looked very dark and dismal that afternoon, and I brought away a very sad picture in my heart of the beautiful Queen being beheaded. I am happy to know that in our country there has never been a Queen so cruel as to murder her first cousin.

One evening at dinner, during our stay in London, the Duke of Manchester sat next to me, and the conversation naturally turned on India and the rapid progress of the country. I was feeling a little sore, as for some unaccountable reason my husband had not been given any Jubilee decoration, and I think I must have let the Duke perceive it. "Well, Maharani," he said, "after all Cooch Behar is a very small State. Surely you don't expect the Maharajah to get a decoration?"

I got rather excited over this. "If a boy goes to school, Duke," I answered, "and does his best but does not get promotion, what encouragement is there for him to work? The Maharajah has done more than any other Ruler to improve the condition of his State, and I think his efforts deserve recognition."

The Duke was amused. "Why don't you talk to the Prince of Wales?" he suggested; "I'm sure he would be delighted at your championship." I must here record that when I arrived in India at the close of my visit, leaving the Maharajah still in England, he cabled that "Her Majesty is graciously pleased to confer on me the

G.C.I.E.;" but although greatly honoured and proud, I was sorry that it was not the G.C.S.I., which I am sure is what H.M. meant to give.

We went to Brighton for a few days for the Goodwood Races. We used to go to the races every day, and enjoyed the drives up the hills much. The first two days the Maharajah was absent; he was paying a promised visit to an old friend. When I met His Royal Highness the Prince of Wales at the races he graciously expressed a wish to be introduced to a cousin of the Maharajah's who was with me. H.R.H. said to my cousin he was sorry the Maharajah was not there; in answer to this my cousin replied that the Maharajah had gone to Leonard's, meaning my husband had gone to stay with Mr. Leonard, but the Prince thought the Maharajah had gone to St. Leonards, and said a few things about that seaside place. The Prince kindly introduced me to Mrs. Arthur Sassoon, a very handsome woman. She kindly asked me to lunch with her, I think at the Prince's request. At luncheon I had the honour of sitting on the left of H.R.H., and I saw a saucer which contained green chillies in front of him.

"Do you like chillies, sir?" I could not resist asking. And the Prince told me he liked nothing better than Indian dishes, a taste acquired, I feel sure, when he paid his memorable visit to our country. That luncheon party was most delightful. The late King Edward had a most wonderful personality. How he remembered things, and how kindly he spoke of India and everything there!

In London I was asked to many dances, and I enjoyed them one and all. They were all full of pretty faces and dresses. The first time I saw Lady Randolph Churchill she wore a perfectly-fitting maroon-coloured velvet dress; I was at the time with Prince George of

Wales, our present King. He pointed out Lady Randolph to me and told me who she was.

My husband and I made a similar mistake at two different dances. At the Duchess of Leeds' ball, I was engaged for a dance to the Earl of Durham. When the dance which I thought was his came, and a gentleman happened to come near me, I asked, "Is this your dance?" the gentleman looked rather amused and said, "You must have taken me for my brother;" he was Lord Durham's twin brother. At another dance we met Lord Abergavenny's twin daughters, Lady Violet and Lady Rose Neville; they were both very pretty and good dancers. My husband was engaged to dance with one, and mistook the other for her.

I went once to a violin concert; I shall never forget it. Dozens of pretty girls dressed in white sat in a gallery and played melodies; the music was beautiful. I went to a very grand dance at Lady Revelstoke's; everything was arranged perfectly, I did so enjoy it. At this dance I was sitting next to Lady when I saw a striking sight: a very tall couple stood at the door at the further end of the room; I had never thought till then that very tall people could ever be very handsome, but when the late Lady Ripon and her brother stood in the drawing-room all eyes were fixed on them, for they were remarkably good-looking.

Lady Abergavenny gave a dance. What a grand sight it was! There were so many beautiful dresses and lovely faces; the music and the supper both were excellent, and the hostess was charming. Lord and Lady Headfort, the present Lady Suffield's parents, were very kind to the Maharajah and to me. Everything was well done, and the hostess's pretty daughters made the bright scene brighter.

One day we went to a delightful afternoon party at Hatfield House. Hundreds of guests travelled down by a special train. When we arrived at the station we found a number of carriages ready to convey us to the house. As I stood there with my husband waiting for a carriage the Maharajah of Cutch, who with his brother was already seated, asked us to get into his carriage. I hesitated a moment, and when I got in, as he is of higher rank than we are, he asked me to sit beside him. I wanted to be next my husband, but the Maharajah of Cutch insisted, and so my husband and the brother sat opposite. In the next day's newspapers we were described as the Maharajah and Maharani of Cutch, accompanied by the Maharajah of Cooch Behar. I was much annoyed, and asked my husband to contradict the report, but he only regarded it as a joke, and said teasingly, "Why, Cutch is much better-looking than I am." After tea the Princess of Wales, who had been talking to me in the gardens, turned to Princess Victoria and said: "Now, Victoria, take the Maharani and show her the Maze. I'm sure she hasn't seen one yet."

I certainly had never ventured inside a maze, but I followed Princess Victoria and Princess Hélène of Orleans unhesitatingly in and out of the winding paths of the labyrinth until we were really lost. We ran screaming deeper and deeper into the maze, and, as "time and tide wait for no man," we realised that we should probably not be able to return to London until very late. We were all wearing dainty muslin and lace gowns; but, regardless of them, we simply broke through the hedges in our search for an exit, and finally emerged with our dresses in ribbons; mine streamed behind me, and the Princesses were in no better plight.

Years afterwards, at King Edward's Coronation, we went to Hatfield again. When we were received by our host, Lord Salisbury, he looked curiously at me. "In 1887," he said, "a Maharani of Cooch Behar came to Hatfield House and lost herself in our maze. You can't possibly be the lady, for you are much too young." I assured him that I was none other, and woman-like I was delighted to know that Time had dealt so lightly with me.

The most appreciated compliment that I think was ever paid to me was uttered as we were returning to town from this garden-party. As we passed through the crowd to our carriage, I heard a woman remark: "Isn't she pretty?"

"Yes," answered her friend, "but it is not only a pretty face, it is also a good face."

The late Lady Salisbury was always very kind to me, and on the night of an India Office party we dined there first, and our hostess took me on with her in her cee-spring carriage. I was talking to her as I got in and forgot the sort of carriage it was, so that I felt very shy indeed as I found myself half lying down. It was largely owing to her kindness that I enjoyed the India Office party enormously. We went to an evening party at the Duchess of Teck's, and there I was introduced to a blind Prince, the Duke of Mecklenburg-Strelitz, the husband of Her late Majesty's first cousin. When I was introduced to him by his wife he paid me a great compliment. "You are looking beautiful, Princess," he said. I asked why he said this. "Because," he answered, "your voice is so lovely."

I was not to leave England without experiencing some of the famous country-house hospitality. We paid a delightful visit to Blair Atholl. The Duke and Duchess were very kind, and I thoroughly enjoyed myself; still I did not find the Scotch scenery half so grand as the mountains of my native land. One day when the Duke was taking Lady Strathmore and me for a drive we passed some white heather, and she exclaimed: "Oh, do stop, there's white heather, the Maharani must have some." The dear old Duke got down from the carriage and dutifully gathered the coveted flowers, while Lady Strathmore explained their mystic properties to me. "Now you will have luck," she said as she gave me a spray. It was the first time I had heard of the superstition, though there are many pretty legends about flowers in India.

One evening we went with the Duchess to a ball, and she decided to go home early. I was tired and asked if I might go with her, and so the Duchess, her sister Lady Strathmore, and I returned to the castle. I had told my maid to leave my door unlocked, and to sleep in the dressing-room, but when we tried to open my door none of us could manage it. One of the ladies therefore went round and woke up the maid, who simply turned the handle and the door was open. We looked at each other with surprise, and as I felt rather nervous the kind ladies had a good search in case there was a burglar. I well remember Lady Strathmore saying: "There are things in this world which our human eyes cannot see." I liked Lady Strathmore, she was such a handsome woman and very clever. I am very sorry I never accepted any of her kind invitations, but I had heard about the ghosts of Glamis Castle. The Maharajah was disappointed, as he was anxious to go and see the old castle, and to shoot, and I deprived him of both these pleasures. At the Blair gathering a very unusual compliment was paid to my husband's dancing; Lady Salterne said: "It is a dream to dance with the Maharajah of Cooch Behar."

At Blair Atholl I heard the bagpipes for the first time, but I am afraid I did not wax enthusiastic over their melody. I look back with pleasure to the time I spent in Scotland. I was treated like a child, and petted and spoilt by every one, and I quite enjoyed the experience.

I went to stay with the Morgans at Cambridge; he was the Master of Jesus College. No one could have received a grander impression of a college than I did. Mrs. Morgan was most kind-hearted, and, I am sure, although she was quite young, she must have helped the students when they were in difficulties. While we were talking our hostess said: "Baby is coming." I asked her who "Baby" was, and she said, "My sister." Soon after "Baby" arrived—the mother of children. It was sweet to hear her elder sister call her "Baby." In the evening a party was given at which we met all the great wise men. None were good-looking nor young, but all were clever, and what interesting talks we had. My hostess afterwards told me some of them exclaimed, "What sparkling eyes!" when they first saw me. The next day was Sunday, and we went to church three times. A boy with a most glorious voice sang by himself; it filled the church and thrilled our hearts.

The Ripons also entertained us at Studley Royal, and there the Maharajah had some partridge shooting. Studley Royal is a fine house and handsomely furnished. I enjoyed my stay there thoroughly. Lady Ripon kindly drove me over to see several interesting ruins. In one, an old building without any roof, I was struck by a fine carving on a mantelpiece of King Solomon's judgment, and I remembered how this story had been told to us by our dear father at the Asram when we were young. One day I went to see Mrs. Vyner, Lady Ripon's mother. On our way we visited a cottage, the home of a ploughman, whose middle-aged wife welcomed us. How interested I was to see it! The little cottage was perfectly clean, there was a small sitting-room, with a few flowers, the paper near the fireplace was white, and I thought it was white marble, there were two little bedrooms, and a kitchen where they dined. A heap of potatoes was under a water-tap, and there was a nice little kitchen garden. Afterwards we drove on to Mrs. Vyner's. Mrs. Vyner must have been a lovely woman in her young days. She sat in her drawing-room all by herself. As we came near the room Lady Ripon most affectionately called, "Darling, are you there?" I was very touched. I was there for some time. Mrs. Vyner's house was furnished with most valuable things. The marble figures and furniture were wonderful. Studley Royal is a picturesque and pretty place; many of the rooms have Indian furniture, and there is a huge stuffed tiger in the hall. In Lady Ripon's town house there is a miniature Indian mud village most perfectly made. We had rather an amusing experience coming back from Ripon. The station officials had omitted to place a "Reserved" notice on our carriage, and at Newcastle a North Country magnate invaded our privacy. I did not like the prospect of travelling with a complete stranger, and my husband politely told the man: "This is a reserved carriage."

"There's nothing to show that it is reserved," he answered.

"But I tell you it is," said the Maharajah. "The omission of the ticket is due to an oversight on the part of the station-master."

"Well, you haven't got an option on the train," the stranger answered rudely, and with these words he began settling himself and his belongings.

"I'm very sorry," said my husband, "but you must get out."

"Must I, indeed? We'll see about that," retorted the intruder. At this moment the Maharajah's valet came up the platform, and, horrified at the annoyance we were being caused, he called the guard, who promptly requested the gentleman to go into another compartment. Looking extremely uncomfortable, he called to a porter to take his dressing-case, and as he hurried away he may have heard my husband say: "I'm really very sorry you are so inconvenienced."

When the Maharajah spoke to King Edward, then Prince of Wales, about our journey and the strange conduct of this man, His Royal Highness was much annoyed.

I could not accept an invitation to Sandringham, as I was in delicate health, and beginning to feel over-fatigued by much travelling. Her Majesty graciously intimated that she wished to be godmother to the expected baby, an honour which we greatly appreciated.

As it was getting cold, the children, in the charge of my brother Profulla, went back to India a few weeks before I did. It was the first time I had an English governess, an English nursery maid, and dear old Mrs. Eldridge. Whether it was fortunate or unfortunate, I do not know, but every English girl I have had in the house has got married in India; even Mrs. Eldridge left me to marry a station-master. My friends used to tease me and say: "Your house is a regular matrimonial agency; if any one wants to get married, they must come to you."

The Maharajah wished to do a little hunting, and as I was going all the way by sea, I left my husband in England. When we arrived at Malta H.R.H. the Duke of Edinburgh came on board to see me, and I much appreciated his kind thought. He talked to me for some time, asked me news of London, and most kindly said he would send his A.D.C. to take me to the Royal Opera that evening, where his box was at my disposal. While we were talking, an old lady, one of the passengers, brought a few flowers for a button-hole, and presented it to H.R.H. How graciously the Duke accepted it, and pinned it on his coat! After the lady had gone I asked the Duke if he knew her, and his answer was "No." This shows what wonderful manners the Royal Princes have; they can make even perfect strangers feel at ease.

On this homeward voyage, I could not help feeling that I was very different from the rather timid little person who had set out on the Great Adventure, and even little Rajey seemed to have become less of a child. "I am a big boy now, I don't want people to kiss me when we arrive in Calcutta," he told his doctor.

On my arrival at Bombay I found my dear mother with my younger sisters and brothers awaiting my arrival; also the Dewan of Cooch Behar and the doctor. What an affectionate welcome I had! My sisters hung round me and caressed me, and we all talked at the same time and laughed; it was too lovely for words. They thought I was looking so pretty, and said that even my hair had grown prettier. Some wanted to brush my hair, others to dress me in pretty saris, and we talked and talked all day and all night.

We stayed only a very few days at Bombay, and then went on to Calcutta. I was received at the station by Sir Henry Carnduff, and every one welcomed me and seemed glad that the visit had proved such a success. Lord Dufferin informed me that the Queen had written to him saying that she was "charmed with the little Maharani," a remark which pleased me immensely. I drove straight to Woodlands, and there I found numbers of friends; we had a special service, and a lovely Indian breakfast. On the following day I went to Lily Cottage, and the welcome I had there I cannot describe. I had a Varan (welcome) ceremony and wonderful meals and congratulations continually pouring in; I don't think any Indian woman ever had or ever will have such a welcome as I had that first time I returned from England. It is a glorious memory to have.

When my husband returned from England he had grand welcome receptions. It is said that such a magnificent elephant procession as he had from the station to the palace had never been seen before. I was not very well and could not accompany him to Cooch Behar. Victor was born on the 21st of May. There were great rejoicings at his birth, which took place at Woodlands; the Maharajah was delighted. We felt it a great honour that Queen Victoria should be his godmother; it was the first time an Indian Maharajah and Maharani had been thus honoured. He was named after her, and Her Majesty sent him a large silver cup. My great regret is that Victor never had the privilege of seeing his Empress godmother.

When we went to Cooch Behar I naturally expected all our people to say something nice to me about our visit to England, and they did, except one man, the Dewan Calica Das Dutt, whose remarks were somewhat like this: "What have they gained by going to England? Instead of having the Queen as godmother to the little Raj Kumar it would have been better if the Maharajah had had some guns."

Victor is the sweetest-natured boy imaginable—most tender-hearted, kind, and unselfish. He adores and worships his brother Jit.

As a little boy he always gave in to Jit; if it was Victor's birthday Jit must have a present too. If Victor went anywhere Jit must go too. They were like twin brothers.

Once at a polo tournament at which I had to give away the prizes, Victor, then a little boy, and who was present with my other children, suddenly disappeared. He had seen a lady sitting in a carriage by herself. He offered to get in and sit with her. "No, dear," the lady said, "you must go and watch with the other children." But Victor insisted: "You are alone," he said, "and I must come and sit with you," and he did. The lady said to me afterwards, "Some day Victor will be a great man." His one desire is to help and to serve others, and he never hesitates to sacrifice his own comfort and happiness in so doing.

When Jit was a little boy my sister Bino had twins, and when he heard it he said: "God has given Bino Auntie those as Christmas presents."

After I returned from England, some English ladies in Simla expected to find me quite spoilt by being so much with the Royal Family and receiving such kindness from them, but I heard afterwards they were pleased to find me otherwise. I certainly began to "live" in a worldly sense. I entertained and was entertained, and I tried to show our Indian ladies that it is quite possible for them to have many social interests and good and true English friends, but I never allowed my devotion to Indian home-life to lessen. When I visited my relations, I sat on the floor as of old, and was one of them just as if I had not left the zenana. Our Indian ladies never weary of listening to the story of my doings in England. "Go on, go on!" they exclaim, whenever I pause to remember something else.

We had a tennis party every week, and sometimes twelve sets going, and always more than two hundred people were invited. Once when the band was playing the National Anthem Jit from the upstairs verandah sang, "God save our gracious Queen." Lady Charles Elliott, who was present, said: "How I wish Her Majesty could hear the little boy! What a loyal little fellow he is!"

About this time my husband lost his step-sister, a very charming lady whose estate was quite close to Cooch Behar. Just before we went to England she wished to adopt one of our sons, but I did not take the suggestion seriously. At her death she bequeathed her property to my husband, who generously gave half to his sister's mother-in-law. Every one was anxious that my husband's share should revert to one of the boys, but the Dewan would not hear of it, and Panga was added to the State. It rested ultimately with Rajey to carry out the popular wishes, and now this State belongs to my third son, Victor.

At a Government House ball I was introduced to the late Archduke Franz Ferdinand. I thought him handsome in a stolid fashion. I had been looking at him with some interest, when to my surprise an A.D.C., came up and told me that His Imperial Highness wished to make my acquaintance. He was duly presented, but was very silent; I soon discovered, however, that he did not know the English language. I afterwards asked my friend the A.D.C. to tell me what remark the Archduke had made. I received this unexpected reply: "H.I.H. said, 'What eyes!'"

I met another charming Austrian, Prince Charles Kinsky, at Government House, and sometimes drove with him. One evening when we were out it grew rather late. Now, I always liked to hear my children say their prayers, and wish them good night, for my home was my paradise, and I was most proud of my nursery. So I told the Prince I must get back, and why. Then we talked about home-life; he seemed so interested in the conversation, and I think he paid me the best compliment that a bachelor could pay. He said: "I hope if ever I marry that my wife will give me as happy a home as you give the Maharajah." His words were so earnest that I wondered if some European ladies had been weighed in the balance and found wanting.

Our mood changed from grave to gay when we discovered that, owing to the high trap and my trailing skirt, I could not manage to get down. Word of my plight was sent to the Maharajah, who was playing billiards. He thought it a great joke, and without any ado he lifted me out and carried me into the home which Prince Kinsky had been praising so much.

Chapter X

HAPPY DAYS IN INDIA

My children led a simple life, and they look back upon it now with happy memories. They used to go out early in the morning for their walk, come back and have their baths, then their simple breakfast, then lessons, after which they dressed and went out for a drive. When they returned, they had a sing-song, supper, and bed. They were most cheerful children, and beautifully unselfish. I hope my readers won't think I say this because I am their mother, for one and all of my friends used to say, "What perfect manners these children have!" They were taught riding by an Australian, named Oakley, who was in charge of my husband's stables; he was very proud of their efforts.

Rajey was a beautiful boy, always a little reserved. He was very fond of horses, and was taught to drive when quite small. He learned high jumping and steeplechasing, and never minded the falls. He was so brave, and perhaps for that reason he was most admired. He thought a doctor could do so much good to poor people. Once he got a little homœopathic medicine case, and used to give the servants medicine when they needed it. He loved his eldest sister and was very proud of Jit. These three were very good friends, and Rajey used to take great care of Girlie. Nurse used to say that Rajey often asked such questions about heaven and the stars, such very strange questions, that she once said to me: "I wonder if that boy will live long?"

Jit was a loving little boy. He was the most spoilt of them all because he had such winning ways. He used to play conjuring tricks when a very small boy. The drawing-room full of people had to look very solemn while he performed these tricks. He would tell his audience to shut their eyes, and he would go and hide something. He would come back, saying: "Open your eyes and see, I have nothing in my hands." We had to close our eyes again while he fetched back the hidden toy, exclaiming: "Now open your eyes and see, I have something in my hands." These were his childish games, and now he is quite clever at conjuring tricks.

Jit used to call me "Dearest." Once in Darjeeling, while I was in the nursery with the children before they went to bed and we had been talking of people sleeping under trees before houses were built, one of the children asked: "Who built the first house in the world?" and Jit answered: "Of course, God built the first house." One of the younger ones objected: "But He has no hands." Jit answered: "But the idea of building came from God."

Vic was patient and good. I remember his once sitting in my room in a corner; I was talking to nurse, when suddenly it struck me that Vic was there, and nurse went and brought him to me. He was cutting his fingers instead of his nails, which he must have seen some of us doing, and the fingers looked so sore; the nurse had not the heart to scold him, and how good he was—not a tear, and they must have pained him much. Victor is the biggest of my four handsome sons.

Mrs. Eldridge ruled our nursery for sixteen years, and she was of more importance there than myself. The children loved her.

The boys and girls were all musical, and it was customary for our friends to drop in at bedtime and listen to the children singing. Very pretty they looked in their sleeping suits. I always dressed them in English clothes.

On the 1st July, 1890, my little darling Hitty was born. Just before his arrival I was very ill; it was a severe kind of influenza, and Dr. McConnell was asked to come down from Darjeeling; my dear husband thought I was seriously ill and wanted special medical advice. Hitty was a fine boy with most glorious eyes; he was the only one born in Cooch Behar. When I brought him to Calcutta we travelled almost the whole way by boat, as it was during the rains, and most of the country was under water. We arrived in Calcutta rather late in the day, and I foolishly gave my baby a bath, and it was this I am sure which gave him a severe cold that turned to double pneumonia. The doctor said he had never seen so young an infant with this severe kind of pneumonia. But he got over it, and I told my husband I would follow him to Simla after I had taken the baby to Darjeeling, where the other children were, as I could not trust him with any one but our dear old nurse. I sent everything on to Simla, but when I got up to Darjeeling, I found it too difficult to tear myself away, and in the end I did not go to Simla at all, which put my dear husband to great inconvenience. For the first time I broke a promise, and for this I shall ever feel regret.

From Cooch Behar we went up to the hills for the rainy months. The rains are very trying in Cooch Behar; all the rivers and tanks are flooded, and the insects! I don't think my Western readers will believe it, but we have more than a thousand different kinds of flying insects; and since we have had electric light they have been worse than ever. My husband used to have dinner inside a sort of mosquito curtain room in order to escape from the pests.

Later on we went to Darjeeling almost every season; first we had the Hermitage, rather a small house where I could not have the English nursery staff, so the children had to be in another house, while the Maharajah and I lived in the Hermitage. When I went over to see the children, very often I would find Girlie and her brothers and some of the staff dressed up and ready to perform little plays and charades for my benefit. Girlie was quite clever at arranging these. She was musical, too, and the Maharajah used to say he sang best when Girlie played his accompaniments.

Sometimes we went to Simla; we had four houses there called Kennedy House, which was supposed to be the oldest house in Simla, and had been Government House. Kennedy House was situated on a ridge and had one of the finest views in the place. One of the houses, known as Rose-bank, has been pulled down and the railway station now stands in its place. I do not know for what reason Lord Curzon, when Viceroy, insisted on my husband selling this property. It could not be because a Maharajah is not allowed to have property in Simla, as other Maharajahs have houses there. It will always be a problem to me and to others. This property was sold for so little money that it was almost given away. Also, when my husband was a minor, the Bengal Government bought from him the present Government House in Darjeeling, for a steam launch and a few thousand rupees. To this day we do not know why it was sold for so little money, especially considering the Maharajah was a minor.

My husband thought a great deal of the elephants, without which no Indian ruler's establishment is complete. The Pilkhana at Cooch Behar is under the management of a State Superintendent, and in 1900 fifty-two elephants were installed there. I have known eighty to be used at a shoot. The huge animals are beautifully trained, and are so intelligent. The Maharajah always fed his own elephant with bananas and bread. The faithful animal knew his voice.

On days of rejoicing the elephants are much used, and their heads are painted in gay patterns. It is a strange sight to see them salute with their trunks. The Cooch Behar elephants are almost pets, if such a word can be used of such huge creatures, and we often used to give them fruit and rice when we met them in the palace grounds. We Indians think more of our elephants than of any other animal, and they have always played an important part in the pageants of our country.

My husband loved animals. I remember once how he tenderly comforted an unfortunate kitten whose plaintive cries could not at first be located. The Maharajah directed that the little animal was to be found, and after a long time it was discovered locked up in the high gallery round the dome of the Durbar Hall. When the frightened little thing was caught, it was half mad with terror. My husband took it into the billiard-room, and sat nursing it, until it quieted down and was able to lap the milk offered it. He kept the little animal until it was quite comforted, and then let it go.

Pretty was born in Lily Cottage in the early morning of the 22nd November, 1891. The Maharajah was very pleased the baby was a girl. I was very ill after she was born, and as the doctors found the case hopeless, I was sent to Colombo as a sort of "kill or cure." I did not die, but returned home well and strong. My kind mother and brothers and sisters accompanied me, and I had Girlie too. I was lame, and had to be carried for months; my eldest brother Dada carried me up to the temple at Kandy, where Buddha's tooth is kept. I am sorry we did not see the tooth, but we did not let the priests know of our visit, or rather that we wished to see it. The temple is a fine one, and we were surprised to see so many Buddhist nuns together. They were all young women, and sitting with alms vessels just outside a room where I believe the tooth is kept. Pretty's name is Prativa.

My youngest child is a girl; her name is Sudhira, but she is still called "Baby." She came to us on the 7th March, 1894. Before she was born I was very very ill with pneumonia and pleurisy; nobody thought we would both live; the doctors said to the Maharajah: "Either the mother or the child," and my husband said: "I want my wife," but he was so happy when he found us both alive. The Maharajah spoiled all his children, and this youngest girl he did spoil much; she never would do anything unless she wished.

In many ways we led a very simple life, although when we entertained none of the ceremonial adjuncts were wanting. As a family we were ideally happy, and I loved my little children with the same devotion which I lavished upon their father.

My great delight was to entertain. The Maharajah and I used to sit together long before the season, whether in the hills or in Calcutta, and make out our programme. In the hills we gave one big ball, and two smaller—one poudré and the other fancy-dress—and dinners and luncheons almost every day, unless we dined or lunched out, and I am glad to feel now when I look back to those happy days that nearly every one of these parties was successful. We often gave Indian dinners, when the guests sat on the floor and ate with their fingers. The present Lord Suffield, then Captain Charles Harbord, every time he came, tried to eat with his fingers, but he never was clever at getting his food to his mouth.

Our entertainments were known to be enjoyable. Our grounds in the cold weather were always covered with tents big and small. The polo tournaments were great events, and many of the regimental players stayed with us for them. We generally gave a garden-party to meet Their Excellencies the Viceroy and his wife. I remember on one occasion I had on a pretty blue dress made by Kate Reilly, and Lady Lansdowne admired it, which made me very proud.

Once I went to see a Maharani, the wife of a rich and educated Maharajah. He was a friend of my dear husband's and fond of my youngest son. I sent messages that I wished to pay my respects to Her Highness, but the dear lady was laid up with fever. After a few days a message came: would I mind going to visit her, as she much wished to see me but was still in bed with fever. Of course I went, delighted to be allowed to see an up-country Maharani in private; we seldom get a chance of seeing other Maharanis in their home-life. This was in Simla. I went in a rickshaw. I waited in the drawing-room for a few minutes, and then was asked to go up to the bedroom. Never shall I forget that picturesque scene. At the farther end of the room, on a single bed lay a lovely woman covered with a gold silk brocade quilt; her face was fair and small, and a huge square-shaped diamond was in the middle of a plait that surrounded her head like a crown. Around the bed stood four or five beautiful young girls, some with great fans and each wearing a different coloured sari embroidered with gold and a few valuable jewels; they were all fair with jet-black eyes. I thought I had never before seen so many good-looking girls together. At the foot of the bed was a huge Big Dane dog; it sat so still I thought it was stuffed. I went near, and the Maharani looked prettier than ever as she smiled and talked. The heir came in and stood for a minute with clasped hands—he was a step-son, and was devoted to his stepmother; he told me, "My own mother could not have been more kind to me." I said I hoped Her Highness would soon be well, and then I remarked that the heir's mother, the first Maharani, must have died very young. "She was lucky, I envy her," said the Maharani. I was surprised at this. The Maharani went on, "How happy I would be if I could be like that, but there is no such luck for me—to leave the Maharajah, my husband, and to die a happy wife's death. Would I had such luck." Little did I then guess the sufferings of a widow. It was strange that this Maharani should die a few hours after her husband, and I was told they had the same funeral pyre.

Our shooting parties were the happiest, gayest affairs imaginable. We drove miles from the palace right into the jungle to the place where the shooting camp was pitched, usually on the bank of a river, and it used to be quite like a little town under canvas. We had dining- and drawing-room tents, a large number of tents for guests, and the State band sometimes came out to camp with us. Many guests came to our shooting camps in those happy years, among them Lord Frederick Hamilton, Colonel and Lady Florence Streatfeild, Colonel Frank and Lady Eva Dugdale, Colonel Lumsden, Colonel and Mrs. Baird, Colonel and the Hon. Mrs. Burn, Lady Hewitt, Lady Bayley, Lady Prinsep, the Duke of Sutherland and Lord Pembroke, Lord and

Lady Minto, Lord and Lady Lansdowne, the Count of Turin, Lord and Lady Galloway, Sir Edward and Lady Sassoon, the present Lord Suffield, Lord Ilchester, Lord Hyde, Lord Jersey, Lord and Lady Lonsdale, Mr. Elphinstone, the Pelham Clintons, the Derek Keppels, Prince and Princess Henry of Pless, the late Sir Henry Tichborne, and many others. All these friends invite me to parties when I am in London. Colonel Evan Gordon, who was our Superintendent for several years, used to get nougat and chocolate from Paris, and these we took in our howdahs and while we were waiting for the day's sport, enjoyed the sweets and read novels. I might just mention here that Mrs. Evan Gordon is a true friend of ours. She helped me much in my coming out in English society; her father, old Sir R. Garth, was the first man I went out for a drive with. Mrs. Gordon's sister, Mrs. Pemberton, sent my dear old nurse Mrs. Eldridge out from England, for which I shall ever be grateful to both sisters. Mrs. Gordon had built a little thatched-roof church, and every Sunday Colonel Gordon preached, and all my English staff, and the bandsman's family, which was a large one, joined. It was so nice; I like my staff to keep up their religion.

On one occasion when I was in camp and my husband was out with the shooters, it grew late and got quite dark, and I became very anxious, as there was no sign of the return of the Maharajah's elephants. It grew later and later—almost dinner time—and I asked the engineer who was in charge of the camp, Hari Mohum Chatterjee, to fire guns. After a short time came the welcome sound of their return. True enough they had lost their way; it was a pitch dark evening, and the poor mahouts did not know where they were going.

Those were happy times. We put the cares of State completely aside, and enjoyed every hour with light hearts. Everybody was full of fun and high spirits.

We were usually out eight or nine hours after big game and returned to camp about 6.30 p.m. Then came a refreshing hot bath, dressing for dinner, and a cheery meal partaken of by often no less than twenty shooters.

Later in the evening my husband talked to the "shikari," who told him where to look for big game. We settled the next day's programme, who was to go and with whom, and all was excitement. Outside was the lovely solemn Indian night; the sky of deep sapphire blue lit up with silver stars was like a canopy over our camp, and the soft winds lifted the tent openings as if curious to find out what it was we were seeking in the solitude of the jungle. These were nights of romance, and I always thought the music sounded more soothing than it did in our palace in the capital. In the camp everything was natural, and the best of every one seemed to come to the surface. We were a party of comrades in the truest sense of the word.

Sometimes, when all was still, we heard the tigers roar in the depths of the jungle. My husband's valet once saw a tiger coming down on the opposite side of the river to drink. He said it was a grand sight. The moon was at the full and the huge beast looked splendid as it stood by the swift river.

The tigers used to come so close to the camp in those days that once while the servants were washing the plates after dinner a big tiger passed by. I took my eldest girl when she was quite small to one of the camps, and about midnight we heard tigers roaring, it seemed as if they were just outside my tent. "Mummy," called Girlie, "I am so frightened, may I hold your finger?" and when she held it she was quite comforted; she thought her mother's weak finger was a protection from the tiger's roaring. I remember listening one night to tigers fighting, and very terrifying were the sounds. The roar of the tiger in his forest home is very different from his growl and snarl in captivity.

I was with my husband when I first saw a tiger shot. Just before we left the camp the Maharajah made me promise not to pull his arm nor touch his gun. I promised, but when I heard the tiger and saw our elephant moving his ears, my good resolutions fled, and I began to pull first my husband's arm and then his coat. Even now I can see his amused smile as he looked back at me.

The grass grows very high in the jungle, but it is burned down in patches, usually in February so that the young grass can grow. The jungle was always very fascinating to me; the trees covered with wild orchids, the sweet air, are lovely to look back upon; in those wilds we could read "the book of nature ever open."

We lunched at mid-day under the trees. One day I got off my elephant to look at a little village. A crowd of the villagers had assembled, and one of them begged me, as the "Mother," to honour his cottage with the "dust of my feet." I complied at once, and as I was going in my host lifted the mantle from his shoulders and placed it on the ground, saying as he did so: "Will the 'Mother' stand on this?" When this ceremony was completed his family came to pay their respects. "My home is greatly honoured by the presence of Lakshmi," he said gravely. I was touched by this simple ceremony, and glad to find this village home so clean. There was a garden well stocked with fruit and vegetables. All was happiness and content, and as I looked at the clear flowing river and the background of forest, I felt as near Peace as I should ever be.

One evening I was returning to camp with a friend who had made a very unhappy marriage. He told me some of his troubles, and as the elephant made its way through the jungle we heard the thin, sad notes of a flute. The air was very still. Soon we saw the player, a shepherd, who was standing on a little hill, against the fading light. He looked so peaceful and happy.

As we listened and looked my friend sighed: "Oh, I'd give anything to be in his place."

One season Count Waldstein of Austria came out to see India and do a little shooting; we all liked him very much, he was a most charming boy. He did not seem very strong, but was very keen on shooting tigers. He went out to camp, but came back with fever and the doctors ordered him up to Darjeeling, where the poor boy died. I have since met his mother; her affectionate heart has drawn me nearer to her than hundreds of the ladies I have met, and her love touched me. I prize her letters more than I can say.

Sir Benjamin Simpson, who was one of the guardians of the Maharajah, took many photographs of the shooting-parties at Cooch Behar. An English maid, after she left me, was staying in a house in Scotland and said she saw some of the pictures on the films, to her surprise. An Englishman has published a book about his shooting in India, and has put into it as illustrations many of the photographs of our shooting camps, calling them his own! The amusing part is that the Maharajah's guests, A.D.C.'s, and staff are in the groups, which the gentleman could not alter.

In our shoots tigers, rhinoceros, buffaloes, leopards, panthers, bears, bisons, boars, and deer of all kinds fell before the guns, and made a grand "bag" at the end of the day's sport. Once when I was out with my husband after rhinoceros, some wild orchids attracted my attention, and I cried out longingly, "Can't I have some of those orchids?" The Maharajah laughingly answered: "Rhino comes first, Sunity."

I must tell my readers an amusing story. A nobleman of high position often came to Cooch Behar for shooting, and after one of his visits I received a large parcel from Japan containing some very expensive kimonos. I was delighted with them, and thought the parcel came from the earl and his wife, so I wrote to the lady and thanked them. In the meanwhile I got a letter from a friend of ours saying she had sent the kimonos. After some weeks the countess wrote saying she was so pleased I liked the kimonos her husband had chosen.

I am sure there can have been few sportsmen to equal my husband. He was a fine polo-player, good at tennis and rackets, and a wonderful shot; while riding, driving, wrestling, and dancing seemed to come naturally to him. His voice was sweet, and he looked his best in his national dress. I remember Lord Dufferin once remarking, when he saw him in full dress, "Maharajah, you do your country credit." My husband had a great desire to make Indian boys keen about sport, and started football for them at Cooch Behar. If he had a weakness, it was his kindness to others.

Although he was progressive in his ideas, the Maharajah never approved of our ladies coming out too freely. He disliked women who smoked and drank with men. He used to say: "India has not yet arrived at the stage when her women can mix freely with men." I have often heard him declare that unchecked Indian youth is far worse than that of any other country. If he saw a girl with rouged cheeks and reddened lips, he would say: "You must never make yourselves look common by painting your faces. God gave women their good looks. Don't use Art."

This ruler, whom so many envied for his wealth and worldly state, was at heart the simplest soul. He was perfectly happy when we were alone in Cooch Behar. In the hills we often cooked together on Sundays in our special kitchen. My husband made vegetable curries, while I was busy with the sweets. My boys and girls also cooked. Sundays were eagerly looked forward to by all of us.

After dinner we had music and played cards. Had any one dropped in then they would have found our house was not that of a Royal Monarch, but of a happy father and husband surrounded by his loving wife and children.

Chapter XI

EDUCATION OF THE BOYS

Rajey's education was at first entrusted to governesses, but in Lord Lansdowne's time, when he was about eleven, we had to settle where he should go to school. There is a college in Rajputana, founded by Lord Mayo and known as Mayo College, where only the Rajput and up-country Princes were educated; no Bengal Prince had the privilege of going there, whether the Maharajahs in that part did not wish it or whether there was any caste prejudice I cannot say. However, Lord Lansdowne kindly arranged that Rajey should be sent there, and Colonel William Lock, the principal, gave my son a cordial welcome.

Mr. B. Ghose was appointed Rajey's private tutor. Oh, how I felt that first parting! I knew that Rajey must be trained for the duties of his position, yet I dreaded giving him over to others. As I bade him farewell at the Calcutta railway station, I was amazed to see how "grown-up" he had suddenly become. He was self-possessed and quiet, yet how loving. As I kissed him, trying to be calm and cheerful, I felt the child was taking his first real step in life. I see him now, the dear face, the loving eyes. There was such perfect understanding between us that a look was sufficient to tell me of what Rajey was thinking, and it is the mother's triumph over death that the love between us still exists and that he is nearer than ever to me now.

I heard that on the night of his arrival Rajey felt the cold exceedingly and was quite ill. "Won't you go to bed?" asked Mr.

Sen, the late Dewan who went with him. "No … no …," replied the child firmly, "it might hurt Colonel Lock's feelings." Rajey was so considerate. He never liked to inflict pain upon any one.

Rajey was very popular at Mayo College. He studied well, and entered into all kinds of sports with zest. His hobby was engines and engineering. He was wonderfully clever in anything connected with mechanics; he used to say: "When I am grown up, I will be an engine-driver. I will get Rs.20 pay and I will give Rs.18 to Hookmi (a favourite servant) because he is so much older than I, and I will keep Rs.2 for myself." He was also very fond of playing at fighting and building forts. He built one in our Calcutta Palace garden and another in the Cooch Behar Palace garden which still exists.

In 1894, Rajey was removed from Mayo College, and I knew I had to face a longer separation from my first-born. It was very difficult at the time of my son's education to know how the young Kumars and future rulers of India were to be trained and where. Some said an English education would not be good for these boys. Others said everybody under the British Empire should learn English and be educated in England if possible, as it fitted them for work of any sort in life. There was much discussion on the subject. The Maharajah decided on education in England, because he had great faith in the discipline of the great English public schools.

When I heard that it was decided Rajey should go to England to complete his education, I thought I would speak about it to the Lieutenant-Governor Sir Charles Elliott. I opened my heart to him and said that it was not right to take young Raj-Kumars away from their country and people. "I believe in home influence. I do not like the idea of Rajey's going such a great distance away from all of us; and he such a homely boy."

But Sir Charles Elliott told me: "There is no college in India like an English public school; it will do your son good, and you will not regret having sent him." I told him: "It will be very hard for the boy when he returns from England to be content with the people of Cooch Behar, who are so backward." And I also said: "How can you expect the boy to keep well in the Cooch Behar climate after being out of it for so many years? It may not agree with him when he comes back."

Somehow nobody took much notice of my remarks and suggestions. But strangely enough when Lord Curzon was Viceroy I heard remarks made by him "that the Cooch Behar boys were too English, and it was hard on them to have been sent away from Cooch Behar when they were so young."

It was disappointing that such a remark should have come from a clever Viceroy like Lord Curzon. If he had made inquiries he would have found it was from a Lieutenant-Governor that the advice had come.

I have often thought what a pity it is we have no Indian Eton, where our boys could be educated without being cut off from their home life. For our boys love their homes and can have no home-life in England. Many Indian mothers have a horror of an English education and think that ruin is bound to overtake their children once they set foot in London.

I am of opinion that my people do not require a Western education. People seem to forget that thousands of years ago India produced astronomers, poets, and sages, when most of the European races of to-day were cave-dwellers. I feel hurt when I hear or read remarks about the bad taste we are supposed to display in our rush after English ideas. Boys who are educated in England do not always get the chance of seeing the right and bright side of English Society, and perhaps get married to girls who are not of their class. I do not blame either the Indian students or the Government for the troubles that have arisen, but as a mother I beg of the English people to go thoroughly into the whole matter before they judge the students.

Rajey was, I think, the first Maharajah's son to receive an English education. "I want my sons to be brought up just as ordinary boys, not as Indian Princes," was my husband's often-repeated wish, and I think he imagined that England would do the best for them. In May, 1894, Rajey and his father left India and I did not see my son again for nearly four years. On their arrival in England, the boy was sent to Mr. Carter's Preparatory School at Farnborough.

If Rajey was home-sick he did not say so, and I was happy to know that he made some very nice friends, amongst them Prince Arthur of Connaught. The Duke and Duchess were most kind to the little exile, and often invited him to spend his holidays with their Royal Highnesses at Bagshot. From there Rajey wrote: "I have a room to myself, a table of my own, a penknife, a pen and pencil on the table." I shall always be indebted to them for their kindness.

Rajey entered Eton in 1897, and was in Mr. Durnford's[1] house. He became very popular with the boys. An old Etonian told me that my son possessed the most beautiful character, and that "no boy was ever more beloved than Rajey."

From the age of twelve till he was sixteen my son was separated from me. I think it was most unkind the way in which the State officials prevented me from going to England to be with my boy. Every time the question was raised, they made the excuse of money difficulties, which I know for certain did not exist. I beg of all Maharani mothers in India that, if ever they are confronted with the same trouble, they will be firm, uphold their own judgment, and not allow the officials to interfere with their home-life. It is cruel to part the heirs when they are so young from their mothers. Now I think it was perhaps a waste of time to educate a ruler's heir in England. The Maharajah did what he and the Government thought best at the time by sending our boys to England for a thorough English education, but afterwards the boys felt their lack of knowledge of the Indian languages very much. They returned home knowing Greek and French, but they did not know Sanscrit or Urdu and found it difficult to speak freely and fluently in the Cooch Behar language. I think there should be Sanscrit teachers in England as well as teachers of Urdu and Bengali; Sanscrit is the most ancient language, and with a knowledge of it one can read and learn much that is most helpful. The heir to a State should have a more general education than the other sons; he should have some knowledge of law, engineering, accountancy, and agriculture, otherwise he cannot improve his State nor help the officials. The education of a Maharajah's younger sons, too, is a difficulty. A Maharajah is not allowed to buy any lands in British districts. I do not know what the reason of this is, but I think I once heard that if the sons of a ruler or his servants commit any crime they cannot be tried by British law because of the Maharajah's own laws, which may account for it. This comes very hard on the younger sons; they can never make themselves rich nor independent. They have to live on their father's estate on whatever allowance the heir is pleased to give them after their father's death. I do not see why a Maharajah's younger sons cannot buy lands in British districts and be independent.

We lost our dear mother in 1898, and I do not think she was sorry to go. The time of separation from my father had been a period of continual sorrow to her, and Death was a friend who re-united them. Her beautiful face wore a smile and she looked like one asleep dreaming of happiness. We could not wish her back again, although our hearts were aching at her loss.

After my mother had passed away my unmarried sisters lived with my brother Saral at Lily Cottage. Saral said: "Unless my sisters marry I shall remain single, and I shall not accept any post that will take me away from them." Although he was younger than my third sister he took care of them like a guardian. He simply lived for his sisters and they one and all adored him. Eventually he married a Miss Sen of Rangoon and built a little house in the grounds of Lily Cottage. This brother of mine nursed my husband in his last illness, for which I shall ever be grateful to him.

The question of Girlie's marriage came up in 1899, and we realised for the first time what difficulties might arise over it. No Maharajah except my husband was a professed Brahmo, and as our rulers have more than one wife, it was impossible to find a husband of her own rank for our daughter. But Mr. Jyotsna Ghosal, of the I.C.S., a member of one of our best Bengali families and a grandson of Maharshi Tagore, proposed for her and was accepted.

As Jyotsna is a civilian, he could not get leave long enough to go to Cooch Behar, so, to the great disappointment of the State people, the wedding had to be at Woodlands, our Calcutta house. Invitations for the wedding were sent to a great number of English officials and friends, and the ceremony took place on the 29th November, 1899, in an enormous tent in the grounds of Woodlands, and three of our missionaries married the young couple. Girlie wore a red and gold sari and was literally covered in jewels from head to foot. She was nearly sixteen, a lovely young girl with the sweetest disposition; the bridesmaids wore white and gold, and my husband and the boys looked splendid in their national costumes.

Jyotsna looked very nice in eau-de-nil Benares silk, and every one remarked how picturesque Girlie looked, and what a happy future seemed in store for her. Cooch Behar was illuminated in honour of the wedding; prisoners were released; life pensions were granted, and remissions of revenue. In the tent there were thousands of seats and hundreds of our English friends sat there, while on the raised platforms the bride and bridegroom, the three missionaries, the Maharajah, and the boys were seated. Girlie had numerous wedding presents; hundreds of beautiful saris, English and Indian silver sets for dinner, tea, and toilet, and lovely jewels from the Maharajah and friends. After the wedding was over about eight hundred guests had dinner together, even the drivers of the carriages each and all had dinner given to them in an earthenware pot tied up with muslin, and next day Girlie went to her father-in-law's house. The parting was sad, but she was so young and pretty we all expected her to be happy in her new home. On the third evening was the flower ceremony and we sent presents, carried by about five hundred men. Girlie's mother-in-law had been one of the most beautiful girls in India; she is very clever and is one of the younger daughters of the Maharshi Tagore and sister to Sir Rabindra Nath Tagore. Girlie has two sisters-in-law, but Jyotsna is the only son and adored by his parents. They welcomed Girlie with great rejoicings and all her new relations are very proud of her. We knew Jyotsna to be absolutely trustworthy, and after twenty-two years I can still say that I could not wish for a better son-in-law.

In 1900 Rajey was at Oxford, and the younger boys at Eton and Farnborough. All my boys, while in England, made numerous friends. Had it not been for the kindness of these friends, I should have been more unhappy and anxious about my boys being so far away from their home. Rajey was much admired, and had he not been so reserved in character he might have been quite spoiled.

Those who knew them at the Preparatory School and Eton have been their best friends. I can never express my gratitude to some of these friends. Long before I had the pleasure of knowing any of them, they used to ask my Rajey to go and spend the holidays with them. Mrs. Nicholas Wood is one of these friends, she has been kind to all my boys. Jit once said: "She is my adopted mother."

Lady Amir Ali, whose husband was a judge out here, asked Rajey once to come from Eton to lunch with her in London. Rajey had leave to go, dressed himself nicely, and came up to town; but when he arrived in the street, he found he had forgotten the number. He walked up and down the street several times, stopped at several houses, but in vain, and had to return to Eton, disappointed and hungry.

After a short time at Oxford Rajey returned to India; he was growing up and the Maharajah was anxious to have his son with him, to help in administrative work and to take a prominent position in the State. It was a splendid idea. It would have brought father and son together in close comradeship with a common interest, and Rajey could have assumed a definite position in Cooch Behar. To my great disappointment, I found that the Viceroy wished Rajey to join the Cadet Corps. This Cadet Corps was started by Lord Curzon; no commissions, no prospects, and no position were attached to it; it could not even be called the Army. The Maharajahs' sons lived in some ordinary buildings like a barrack. One day Rajey, who had been thus forced to join, was out walking when he passed the General and the Commanding Officer. Afterwards the C.O. was much annoyed with him because he had not made a proper salute to the General. Rajey answered: "But, sir, I could not make a military salute because the General was not in uniform." The C.O. was, I believe, in a rage, but he was wrong and my son was right; evidently the C.O. did not know the Army regulations. Later, Jit and Victor followed Rajey into this corps.

Most unwise remarks were made by the Dewan and Superintendent about Rajey learning administrative work. The Dewan said bluntly that there was nothing for the Maharaj Kumar to learn. The Superintendent told me the Viceroy wished Rajey to devote himself to the Cadet Corps until he was twenty-six years of age, and then he might return to the State. I was amazed and could not understand why the heir should be made to stay away from his State and parents so long! But the State people seemed to know more about it. They thought: "The Maharaj Kumar is too clever to be with his father, who is surrounded with such officials as we." One day a major remarked to me: "Well, Maharani, you've sent Rajey into the Cadet Corps. What will he learn? Nothing. You might as well send me." This outspoken comment was the opinion of many.

I wonder why no Viceroy of India has ever given any of our young Princes a place on his staff. It would appeal tremendously to our people and prove that the much-discussed English training meets with its reward. Our Princes mix on terms of equality with Englishmen at the public schools and universities. Yet, in their own land, they are denied positions of honour!

Queen Victoria was loved by the Indians more than people in England have any idea of, and we often expressed the belief that our happiness was due to the reign of a Queen. She was known, and will ever be known, as the "Good Queen." Indian women appreciated the fact that she was a good wife, a good mother, and a good woman all round. When the news of her illness came every one spoke of it with grief. "What shall we do if anything happens to Queen Victoria?" Although they never had the honour of seeing their Queen, all Indian women admired and respected our late Empress, and I well remember when the news came and the guns were fired, how all the ladies said: "We have lost our Mother." How I wished I had seen her once more! My dear friend, Miss Minnie Cochrane, told me that Her Majesty had several times expressed a wish to see me again, and my great regret is that I did not have the honour and pleasure of showing my Victor to his godmother. When I came over in 1902 I went to see her mausoleum at Frognal, and I wrote a few lines in Bengali, tied them to a wreath, and presented it. I had brought the children with me on this visit, and first of all rented Moor Hall, a country house between Battle and Bexhill; but the place disagreed with us, and the slow train service completed our disenchantment. We came up to town, and in the winter I went to Switzerland with the girls. We stayed at Territet and Villeneuve.

The latter I thought was pretty, and some of the old villages were rather like India with their brick buildings and stone steps; but no scenery in Europe ever appeals to me like that of my own country.

As the Maharajah was coming over shortly for King Edward's Coronation, we returned to London viâ Paris, and I rented Ditton Park, a lovely place between Slough and Datchet. The King had given a house in Lancaster Gate to my husband as his guest and aide-de-camp. That summer is one of my happiest recollections. The children were all growing up. Two of the boys were at Eton, and the youngest at Farnborough. Rajey was the dearest companion, and most devoted son that ever gladdened a mother's heart. What more had I to wish for?

I remember a wonderful toy railway, lines, tunnels, hills, and everything in miniature, which the boys constructed in the park, and I opened this "Ditton Park Route" with great ceremony. Then came the mania for cricket, when every one played most of the day, and a cart conveyed lunch to the teams. The boys' friends often came from Eton without leave on Sundays—luckily they were not expelled— and revelled in curry teas. It was all light-hearted merriment and one perpetual romp. They had to fly back to college; sometimes it got late and my third brother had to drive them back, and they always sang: "Good-bye, Sally, I must leave you." How happy Jit and Victor were! How I had struggled to avoid parting with the boys when they first went to school, but seeing them so happy with so many nice little friends my heart bowed down with gratitude that they should be Eton boys. Even now when they meet their Eton friends they speak happily of their college days. My poor darling little Hitty was the one who most wished to stay at home; not that he was unhappy at school, but he loved being with me. When he came home for the week-ends, every time I saw him off in the train big tears would roll down his cheeks and make my heart ache till I saw him again. And now he has gone and left me to weep over those days of my happy past.

When news came that, owing to the King's illness, there would be no Coronation, London wore a most miserable aspect; I don't think I have ever seen anything to equal it. But when our beloved Monarch rallied and recovered, the sad time of doubt and danger through which the nation had passed, was quickly forgotten.

When I was having my hair dressed to attend the Coronation ceremonies the attendant said to me: "Perhaps some day the Kaiser will be King of England." I asked her why, and she said: "Because he is the son of the Queen's eldest child, and ought to be the heir." I could not help laughing at the idea, and said: "England can't be Germany; it will always be England."

I went to the Coronation with Rajey, who had a very unsuitable seat among the tradespeople, owing to some regrettable oversight. He looked beautiful in white with many jewels. My husband rode in the procession as one of King Edward's A.D.C.'s. We were invited to the party at the Foreign Office, and Rajey was in attendance on the present King, and wore British uniform. His complexion was fair, and I remember some of my lady friends in the gallery did not at first recognise him. He had recently been appointed to a commission in the Westminster Dragoons.

I stood between Princess Frederica of Hanover and Princess Henry of Pless, and people remarked on the contrast between us, as Princess Frederica had the loveliest grey hair and Princess Henry of

Pless beautiful fair hair, and my locks were raven black. I heard that my tiara was voted the prettiest there.

The review held at Buckingham Palace was a wonderful sight. Three times a message was sent that I should take a position near Her Majesty. I hesitated, thinking there must be some mistake. As we waited on the terrace, the King came up and shook hands with me, and Queen Alexandra asked me to follow her to the tent in the grounds. When we entered I was directed to sit near His Majesty, and felt most nervous all the time. I was thinking somebody had made a mistake when they put me in that seat of honour.

After the presentation of medals to the troops, His Majesty rose and handed me something, saying a few words as graciously as he alone knew how to speak. The "something" was the Coronation Medal, and as I was the only lady to whom one was given, I was touched and very much overcome, as I curtsied and expressed my gratitude. I remember how amused the Prince of Wales (now our King) was when the colour came off the red-covered boxes of Coronation Medals which he was giving away. At the finish his white gloves were stained vivid crimson, and he and the Grand Duke of Hesse regarded the effect of the faulty dye as a huge joke.

The Court was gorgeous. I had a handsome dress made by a French milliner for the occasion. The heavy gold embroidery was unique; it was very like the Delhi embroidery and was much admired. I believe I looked rather nice, as an old friend said: "The Maharani looked her best." The Princess of Wales, our present Queen, liked the dress very much, and thought it was a piece of Indian work. Both Their Majesties spoke graciously to me when I made my deep curtsies. A message was sent from Lady Lansdowne, who was next the King, that Their Majesties wished me to stand in the front line so that I might have a good view of the ladies passing. I was most grateful and impressed by the kind thought of Their Majesties. I often wondered how their royal minds remembered so many little things.

At the grand State Ball after King Edward's Coronation one of the ladies, very handsomely dressed, had forgotten to fasten her waistband; I felt most uncomfortable seeing this, and longed to tell her but did not like to. Her appearance was magnificent, but to my mind quite spoiled by the two strips of ribbon with hooks hanging down.

We lunched with Their Royal Highnesses, the Connaughts. It was one of the most enjoyable parties to which I have been asked.

I went to a party at Lady Warwick's and stayed the night, and I found her as clever as she is handsome and a most charming hostess.

We went to one review, at which we had seats somewhere right away. I was touched when some of the Princes saluted me in the distance. It pleased my Rajey. I also went to the Duke of Westminster's dance.

Shortly after, a polo team was to go from England to Trouville. My husband could not get away from his duties as the King's A.D.C. and Rajey was to play for his father in the team. I am not usually superstitious, but I had misgivings about this journey. The morning Rajey was leaving for Trouville it was cold and foggy. When he came to say good-bye I told him that perhaps the crossing would be very rough and unsafe. He only laughed. Within a short time after he had started I heard his voice on the stairs, and he came in and said: "Mother, I just missed the train." Then I exclaimed: "Oh, darling, don't go; your missing the train shows you are not to go to-day." But he would not listen to this. He started by a later train. And that day's dark fog brought him ill luck and from that trip his health was never the same.

One day, when I was walking in the garden at Ditton, I received a telegram from a friend who was at Trouville that Rajey was "getting better." Why! I did not even know that Rajey was ill. What did the telegram mean? Then my husband broke the alarming news that my son had had a dreadful fall at polo, but luckily the pony stood still and he had escaped worse injury.

I shall always be grateful to our kind friends, the Hays, for all they did for my Rajey while he was at Trouville.

The French doctors' treatment has always been incomprehensible to me. For days during Rajey's period of unconsciousness they kept him on nothing but champagne. When he was able to be moved, my son was brought to London, and the specialists whom we consulted gave their opinion that he had not sustained any injury to his head, but my husband was not satisfied and felt something was wrong.

We went to Lowther Castle to stay with Lord and Lady Lonsdale. It is a fine castle with very pretty gardens. I admired the rock gardens. One thing I saw there which I shall never forget and I am grateful to Lord Lonsdale for having shown it to me, and that is the blue lotus. It blooms in the evening and closes in the day. It is an extraordinary thing that in the Hindu mythology it is written that when Ram Chandra went to Ceylon he worshipped his goddess with the blue lotus, and since then it has never been seen or heard of in India. When I told my people in India that I had seen the blue lotus they were so interested and begged me to try and bring it to them.

Lord Lonsdale said he got it from America, and promised to send me a plant, but it has not yet come. Rajey, who was with us, was too ill to enjoy the visit, and our friends declared that his proper place was a darkened room and a rest cure.

After a stay of a few weeks I had to return to India for the arrival of my first grandchild, and to make preparations to take part in the great Durbar at Delhi. When I arrived in Calcutta I found Girlie suffering from a very high fever; Woodlands looked like a nursing home; nurses and doctors were everywhere, and it was a depressing atmosphere. I watched my child, and instead of getting better she grew worse. One day, I do not know what made me think of it, but I suddenly determined to take my child away to the hills. It was very cold, and the doctors were horrified at my suggestion, but I took Girlie, first to Kurseong, which is not so high, and afterwards to Darjeeling, which was quite deserted, and I am thankful to say within a few days she got better.

I now began to think about the Durbar. I heard that all the Maharanis present were to be in purdah, and I decided to follow their example, but my husband told me, unless I was given my rightful position by his side, he would not take me.

Rajey, who was seriously injured internally, had such a wonderful constitution that he looked neither ill nor sad, although he was in the hot sun for hours at the Durbar. It was a magnificent sight, and I shall never forget the display of jewels worn by our Princes. There were emeralds of a wonderful deep green, priceless pearls, rubies like blood, and diamonds dazzling in their brightness; in fact there were jewels everywhere, even the elephants were decorated with them. I saw a Maharajah whose gold fan was fringed with beautiful pearls. I shall never forget the elephant procession; it would have been a perfectly joyful occasion but for a misfortune. Mrs. H. M was staying with me in our camp at the time, and as I had not received a card the Maharajah did not wish me to go. Mrs. M, on hearing this, said she would make it all right for me, she was certain to be able to get a card from Sir H. Barnes, who was an old friend of hers, and I must go. When the morning came, however, there was still no card and I said I would not go, but Mrs. M pressed me hard; she was bent upon my going, and against the Maharajah's wishes I set out with her. The result was that in the end we made quite a sensation among the crowd. My coachman was directed by Mrs. M, and we drove on and on and turned from one road to another and often drove back, as after a time on certain roads no carriage was allowed to pass. Mrs. M stopped the carriage dozens of times to ask the mounted policemen where Sir H. Barnes was, but no one gave her satisfactory answers; we went past the same places over and over again. Many of my friends, relations, and acquaintances saw me and wondered what had happened. It got late and the policemen said we must alight as carriages were no longer allowed to be there. Several times I told Mrs. M I wished to return to camp, but she would not hear of it. We went near the Masjid—the place where English ladies gathered to see the procession. Mrs. M wanted me to wait till she found Sir H. Barnes. The sun was hot, and I felt frightfully insulted and hurt. Some people who were there asked me to go up the steps, which I did. When I got inside I tried to smile, but I felt more like crying. I met some of the Viceroy's A.D.C.s and told them that I had gone there without a card and felt nervous. Instead of offering me a chair or saying something to ease my mind they walked away. Thus that most enjoyable sight, the elephant procession, is stamped on my mind as "a sad experience."

Lady Curzon looked very handsome in her splendid dress. The cheers with which Their Royal Highnesses the Duke and Duchess of Connaught were greeted can never be forgotten. Lord Curzon made a grand speech, really I felt that I could scarcely tire of listening to him, he is such an eloquent speaker.

In 1904 Rajey was taken ill. Our own doctor diagnosed the complaint as remittant malaria, a complaint of which I had not heard. He became rapidly worse, and in despair I wrote to my husband, who was in Darjeeling, and told him that I thought Rajey ought to have the best advice in Calcutta. When consulted, the Calcutta physicians declared that the opinion of a London specialist was necessary, as Rajey's heart was affected. He was ordered to England at once, but needless to say he was not allowed to go until he had received leave from the Cadet Corps. It was monsoon time and my poor boy went alone. Afterwards I found out to my intense annoyance that our Superintendent had written privately to the Calcutta doctors, asking if the Maharaj-Kumar were actually ill, or merely gone to England to enjoy himself. The doctors were furious at this, and did not mind telling the Superintendent so. One of them said: "Does he think I'm open to a bribe?" This trivial incident shows what used to happen when our personal affairs were in question, but I am happy to say this state of things is gradually being changed. My darling son was not allowed to go in search of health without being exposed to the insult of suspicion, and mud thrown in this manner sticks. It is impossible not to feel some bitterness over the many cruel rumours which are entirely without foundation. Let a ruler or prince have but the slightest failing, it is instantly magnified fourfold and discussed unmercifully, without a single attempt to counterbalance it by any remembrance of the victim's better qualities.

I have been obliged to sit and listen to falsehoods about princes who were our friends which almost took my breath away, as I realised their cruelty and injustice. I remember one Maharajah in particular who was a very kind man, very "English" and very sporting. He knew us well, and I remember my husband telling me how this Maharajah once saved the honour of an officer. The latter had had a bad day at the races and was thousands of rupees in debt. He was a hard-up, smart Army man, and could not lay his hand on such an amount. What was he to do? The honour of a British officer was at stake. Suddenly he remembered the Prince and sent a despairing message telling him of his plight. The kind Prince paid the debt of honour without a moment's hesitation. When the Prince died later people spoke of him most unkindly and hailed his death as the best thing that could have happened to him.

I always think of that poor Prince in connection with a certain old Sudan legend:

A little village far away in the jungle was smitten with cholera, and the panic-stricken people wanted to put the great stone image of their god into the Ganges until the plague was over. One of the villagers dreamt that the god appeared and told him that his image could only be moved by a man who was pure in heart and loved God. The villager related his dream to the priests, and orders were issued that the people should assemble on the morrow and try to find a man who could carry out the instructions of the god. All tried, the so-called best men, the holy, the strongest, the bravest. But to no avail! The stone image smiled its inscrutable smile in the scented gloom of the temple, and the priests were in despair. At last a thick voice broke the stillness, and the villagers saw a man, whom they all knew to be a hopeless drunkard, come reeling unsteadily into the sacred precincts of the temple. "What's all this I hear about the dream?" he demanded, propping himself up against a worshipper's unwilling shoulder. "I tell you it is quite true. The great god knows who loves him and who loves him not. There's none here who loves him better than I do. So mine shall be the hands to give him to the care of Mother Ganges." He swayed towards the huge image as he spoke, and the horrified crowd thought that some dreadful punishment would fall upon him for such sacrilege.

The drunkard approached slowly; for an instant he pressed his drink-swollen face against the marigold-wreathed breast of the image; then clasping it in his arms, he lifted the idol from its recess as if it were light as a feather, and carried it forth to the bank of the river.

The awe-stricken throng were speechless with amazement that a poor drunkard should be chosen to show them how, under the cloak of failings and frailties, there existed a heart which remained pure, and wherein was to be found "the invisible kingdom of God," which is all truth and all love.

1. Now Sir Walter Durnford, Provost of King's College, Cambridge.

Chapter XII

SAD DAYS

Life went on very much as usual year after year. My children, my duties, and my social interests filled up most of my time. In 1906 I went to England with Jit, Pretty, and Baby, and Rajey joined us later. We lived near Englefield Green at Park Close, where there was a luxurious Roman bath. One day after luncheon I had washed my hair and was sitting drying it when the children came running up: H.R.H. the late Duchess of Connaught and her daughter were in the drawing-room. It was just like her gracious dear self to pay so delightful a surprise visit. I twisted up my hair and ran down and expressed my delight and thanked the Duchess. It was wonderful how she had remembered me and found my address. This kind action perhaps was little to her but it meant much to me.

Our life was peaceful and untroubled, and I was glad to have my children with me. The two girls were growing exceedingly pretty, and I was proud of the admiration they received. I have often been playfully accused of over-indulging my girls, but I was so proud of them that I loved to see them wearing pretty things. Pretty was like a gorgeous damask rose just unfolding to loveliness, but perfectly simple and sweet. Once in Calcutta she was telephoning to Lord Bury, one of the A.D.C.'s, who asked who she was. Pretty said: "Don't you know me? I am Pretty." Lord Bury, whose manners are just what an A.D.C.'s should be, said: "Are you?" One evening at Lily Cottage there was a "jatra." I left Pretty on the terrace, and my sister Bino said to me: "That daughter of yours is beautiful; she looks as if a fairy had dropped her from heaven." Pretty is musical and loving; her weakness is she can never say "no." When she has a grand wardrobe, if any one comes and admires anything, she feels she must make a present of it to her. If she goes to buy a dress, perhaps the dress is unbecoming to her, yet she buys it because the dressmaker wishes her to have it. She keeps her room beautifully tidy, but as far as her dresses go I do not think any girl can be more careless. Once in Simla, when we were there for a few weeks, Lady Minto asked us to a dinner and dance. Pretty was expecting a new dress that evening; as it did not turn up, I told her to put on one of her old ones. She was disappointed but obeyed me. Lady Minto kindly sent her brougham to drive us to Government House, and when we went in to the brilliantly lighted drawing-room an A.D.C. whom we knew very well asked Pretty if she had not any other dress; it looked so old and untidy.

During this second visit to England I was invited to a family luncheon at Marlborough House, at which I was the only guest. It was a happy simple meal. Some of the Royal children were at table, and I remember a dear little boy who played with a book on the floor and ran up to his father now and then to show him a picture. The baby came in with the sweets, and the Princess and I talked about our children to our hearts' content. I shall always remember that happy scene of Royal home life: the Prince of Wales all kindness, the Princess, the ideal young matron, handsome in her fair healthy style, and happy in the possession of her beautiful children. I only wish my country-women could have seen that picture of happy home life, it would have impressed them deeply. We talked about

India and the Indians, and H.R.H. told me she liked everything Indian.

The Prince and Princess of Wales visited India in 1905. During their visit my husband met with an accident at polo, and His Royal Highness sent frequently to ask how he was.

The Princess went to a zenana party at Belvedere, which was attended by ladies of the highest rank. Every one was charmed with their future Queen and she presented us with medals in commemoration of her visit.

Their Royal Highnesses graciously honoured us with their company at luncheon. We had only a few friends present, among them Sir Patrick Playfair, who told me afterwards that the Prince of Wales said they had enjoyed their lunch.

In honour of their visit there was an enormous Indian reception, at which my daughter Baby, looking very pretty and graceful, presented a bouquet: and at the laying of the Foundation Stone of the Victoria Institute both Sir Louis Dane's daughter and Baby presented bouquets to Their Royal Highnesses. I remember an old English gentleman saying afterwards to me: "What a beautiful little girl your Baby is, and how beautifully she made her curtsy! I shall have to wait until she grows up and marry her."

The Cadet Corps was, of course, well to the front on the occasion of Their Royal Highnesses' visit, and I must say that for the first time I was glad it was so ornamental. My boys looked very handsome on horseback in their white achkans, blue belts, and turbans of white, blue, and gold.

The Maharajah, who was in the prime of life, now suddenly lost his splendid health. He had become very thin, and began to look ill, which alarmed us very much, and we decided to go to England and consult the best specialists. In May, 1910, when we arrived in Bombay, the papers were full of startling rumours about the health of King Edward; we already knew from private sources that His Majesty was ill. Just as we were going on board the steamer the news arrived that our beloved Sovereign was dead. We were filled with dismay and sorrow, and I feared the effect the blow would have upon my dear husband in his weak state. The Maharajah had been so specially honoured with the late King's friendship that he lamented his Sovereign more as a beloved friend than as a great King.

The harbour at Bombay looked most solemn and funereal with the flags all half-mast high, and as I said farewell to those left behind I felt terribly sad. The voyage was most gloomy, and I remember that every one discussed the fateful Halley's comet which it was supposed might destroy the earth about the time we should be approaching the coast of Italy. I, woman-like, was nervous at the prospect when I heard it so definitely announced. "My goodness!" I gasped, "we shall all be burnt to death." The Maharajah turned to me with his loving smile: "What does it matter, my dear? I'll hold your little hand and we'll die together."

As we neared the end of the voyage, we discovered we should not be in time to attend our Emperor's funeral. The Maharajah felt this very much, as he had been most anxious to be present and pay his last tribute of respect to his beloved Sovereign. When we reached London how sad everything was; although the funeral was over the shadow of loss was still there. The sight of a nation's grief is overpowering, especially when, as in this case, it is truly sincere.

We stayed at the Hotel Cecil, and my husband received an unofficial intimation that he might go to Windsor and see the last resting-place of the late King. I cannot be thankful enough for the kind thought or sufficiently grateful that we were allowed to pay this last tribute of respect to our friend and Sovereign. My husband and I, my brother Profulla, and one of the A.D.C.s went by motor. It was a sad journey. As I saw the grey towers of Windsor Castle my mind went back to that bright day, years ago, when I paid my first visit there. Time brings changes, and I realised it then. We were received by a dignitary of the Church, whose name escapes my memory, and he led the way to the Royal vault under St. George's Chapel. We descended a flight of stone steps. A door was thrown open and we entered. King Edward's coffin was lying on a raised stone slab in the middle of the vault. A prie-dieu stood near it. I knelt down and burying my face in my hands offered up a fervent prayer. My husband knelt too, and as he prayed he wept. It was touching to see the big man grieving for his King. We placed on the coffin the wreath of orchids we had brought with us. I had written a few words in Bengali on the card attached to it, which translated were:

"With tears of sorrow we present you this, our so Beloved Peacemaker. Your work is accomplished."

The journey back to town was sad. We hardly spoke, for our thoughts were of our dear King in his last resting-place; never again should we see him.

A few weeks later, I received a message that Queen Alexandra wished to see me at Buckingham Palace. The late Lady Suffield welcomed me, and after a few minutes the Queen entered the room.

She was in deepest black, and I thought she looked more spirituelle and lovelier than ever in her mourning. The Queen kissed me and told me to come and sit near her. I felt I could have fallen at her feet and wept as I listened to her simple sad words about her great sorrow and her love for her husband. There was no bitter rebellion against Fate in the Queen's words, but resignation, hope and perfect faith.

"I hardly realise even now that the King is gone, never to come back again," Her Majesty said to me, her large eyes full of tears. "At first I felt as though any moment he might come into the room." I could not speak for tears. "I want you to accept this souvenir from me," and, as she spoke, the Queen handed me a brooch with the entwined cypher, A. and E. "Keep it in memory of our friendship." Her Majesty also gave me a ruby scarf pin which had belonged to the late King and his cigarette case for my dear husband. "He was so fond of the Maharajah, and I hope your husband will wear the pin, the King often wore it," Her Majesty told me.

I am sure Queen Alexandra would be pleased if she knew how much she is beloved by the women of India. I often speak to our ladies about her.

We lost no time in consulting specialists about the Maharajah's health. Dr. Beasley Thorne advised a course of Nauheim treatment in a private nursing home. Luckily the Home in Inverness Terrace was not one of the abodes where sufferers experience discomfort as well as illness. The only complaint my husband made was that he felt lonely. He wrote me that unless I went and stayed with him he would not finish his course of treatment, nor remain in the Home. So I went and stayed there until the treatment was finished.

Dr. Beasley Thorne was like a father to my husband. Even when in great pain my husband's face brightened when he saw the doctor. The Maharajah had perfect faith in this kind man, who was with him till the last. After the treatment the Maharajah went to Whitby, but he had misgivings. "I don't feel really better, although the doctors say I am," he wrote.

Troubles followed us in rapid succession. Baby had to undergo an operation, I lost a very faithful Indian servant, and in October my husband developed pneumonia. We were then living at 28, Grosvenor Street, but afterwards we moved into 2, Porchester Gate. Rajey had arrived in England, and his state of health worried me to distraction. I seemed beset with difficulties and dangers, and did not know what to do for the best.

In February, 1911, I took a small house, 6, Lancaster Gate, where I was ill. As soon as I was able to move I returned to Porchester Gate. Pretty was ill; in fact, it seemed to me that thick clouds were hanging over me and made my path very hard to travel. How difficult it is to smile when one's heart is breaking!

My husband was ill during the Coronation festivities and I did not at all want to go out to parties, but he would not bear of my staying away and had beautiful dresses made for me. It was so hard to have to attend grand State parties when I longed to be at home with him. On the day I went to the Abbey I took my Jit with me, and as my husband was ill both he and I hoped that little Jit would be given a seat near me. Instead of this he was put right away somewhere and I had to sit with all the other Maharajahs. Although this was a great honour, my heart was sad and I longed to have the boy with me.

My husband rallied a little about this time and we went to Court, but his altered appearance excited every one's sympathy. Shortly afterwards pneumonia again set in and he was dangerously ill.

As the Maharajah's medical advisers were of opinion that change of air might work wonders, we decided to go to Bexhill, where we rented a little bungalow facing the sea. The day we left London was marked by an ominous accident. As I waited on the landing, I heard a sudden fall. I rushed up the stairs and found my husband sitting on a stair, he had been coming down when he slipped, missing about five steps. There was a great mirror at the end of the stairs. Had he gone through, the accident might have been a fatal one. "An omen, an omen," said our Indian servants to me. "Why do you take His Highness to-day? it is an unlucky day." It can easily be understood what a shock I received from this mishap. When we first went to Bexhill we were in great hopes that the change would do my husband good. We went for one motor drive, but after that he looked worse and did not care to leave his room. A new doctor was recommended by Dr. Beasley Thorne, a Dr. Adamson, whom my husband appointed civil surgeon of Cooch Behar. He was with us in the bungalow. I was frightened to see how sure my husband felt he would never get well. He was quite prepared to go, and his world seemed rapidly fading away from him. "Let us be happy together. My journey is almost at an end. Why do you fear death?" were remarks he often made at Bexhill.

As I saw him getting more and more ill I spoke to Dr. Thorne and sent a cablegram for my eldest girl and youngest boy to come.

It was a gentle journey towards the Unknown, and the traveller, who had to pass alone, was the least concerned. After hours of pain, my husband's greeting to my brother was: "Hallo, Nirmal, I don't feel very bright to-day." At the answer: "Yes, sir, it's been a brave fight," my husband's face lit up; he loved to feel the victory lay with him.

Neither my children nor those with me realised my agony. They were losing a father and a friend, but I was losing all that made the crown and glory of life, the love of my girlhood, the beloved husband. They understood nothing of this, but he did. I saw it when he looked at me, I felt it as his hand clasped mine, but I knew he wished me to be brave and not hinder his passing.

My sister's son-in-law, Dr. Banerjee, was our family doctor. My husband was very fond of him, and he nursed the Maharajah all through his illness. His wife, my niece, had often cooked curries at Porchester Gate, which my husband had greatly enjoyed.

My boys and my brother Saral and the staff nursed my husband day and night, but it was of no avail. My youngest brother, who had just taken his medical degree, and of whom my husband was very fond, also nursed him. This pleased my dear husband.

One night he was very ill, and I said to my nephew, who was attending him: "You are the one who must save him," and he did give the Maharajah something which kept him for a fortnight or more. Another night the Maharajah talked so affectionately to Jit that the boy left the room and had a good cry outside. On another occasion I went in and found my husband with Rajey on one side and Dr. Beasley Thorne on the other. Looking at me, he said: "I am most happy, and want nothing more." He used to listen for my footstep, and though in great pain and sickness his face always beamed when I came into the room, but he could not bear to see tears in my eyes. My children always said: "Mother, you must not shed any tears before father." It was very hard always to wear a smile when all I longed to do was to fall on the floor and weep, but I had to look cheerful and talk brightly.

He liked having my sister Sucharu near him, and when no one else could persuade him Baby would make him drink barley water or take his food. Once on seeing his father in pain, Rajey cried and said: "I shall not come again, it is too painful to see father in such agony." Perhaps these young people realised then what the loss of their father would mean to them, for his influence had dominated them when my affection had made me weak, and I think he understood them better than I did.

The last words that the Maharajah wrote were on a slip of paper. They were only two words: "Saral … household." Most likely he wished this brother to be always with us. Saral's wife was very good to me.

We had a very good male nurse, Francis. I shall ever be grateful for all his devotion to my husband. My eldest girl and my youngest boy, my brother, and the late Dewan P. Ghose, who was personal assistant to the Maharajah, arrived in Bexhill about a fortnight before the end. This Dewan had been his personal assistant for years.

There was a big picture of my father in my husband's bedroom at Bexhill, and looking at this one day my husband said: "I am a real follower of his." Just a few days before he passed away he said to me: "Sunity, what are your plans?" I said: "My plans are your plans. When you are better we shall return home." Gently he answered: "I know my plans and I would like you to make your plans." At this answer my heart sank. Once he sent for the boys and spoke to them, saying his journey was finished, and told them what he wished them to do. He looked round with such loving eyes just before he breathed his last at all his children, his brother-in-law, and staff; held my hands, calling me "poor girl"; and after saying a prayer, with a smile he quietly passed away. There was no mark of suffering on his face. Suddenly the notes of "The Dead March" of the Rifle Brigade sounded close by. It was in the evening of the 18th September, 1911, at seven, and the band had been playing, but when the news reached them they ended with that sad tune.

I cannot remember much except the agony through which I passed. I heard as one in a dream that messages of condolence had been received from Queen Alexandra, King George and Queen Mary, and hosts of our friends in England and India. But I was overwhelmed with grief. In spirit I was trying to overtake my beloved upon his lonely journey. Naught else troubled me.

I saw my husband lying in his coffin, and I bade him my last farewell alone, before he was taken to London.

Profulla said the Maharajah's funeral ought to be military, as he was a Colonel, and not that of a Maharajah. He sent a message to the Government and His Majesty ordered a grand military funeral. The Coldstream Guards played the "Dead March" and the "Last Post," and both at Bexhill and in London, from Victoria Station to Golders' Green Crematorium, people came in throngs. Even the relations in India said H.H. could not have had a grander or more impressive funeral. His Majesty was most gracious, and for this kind act of his, one and all in Cooch Behar, family, friends, and subjects, will be for ever grateful. The many flowers received with the sympathy of friends, for which I regret to say it was impossible to thank every one individually, were greatly appreciated by me in my hour of darkness.

I remained with my grief at Bexhill, and the duty of committing his father's body to the flames fell upon Rajey. He walked to the head of the coffin as it rested in the Crematorium and mastering his emotion with a great effort, raised his hand: "In the name of God, Almighty Father, I commit these last remains of my beloved father to Your keeping. That in him which is immortal will always live, the mortal dies and perishes in the flames. God, keep and bless him in Your holy care."

The Rev. P. Sen conducted the last service, which I heard was most impressive; and some of my English friends told me afterwards they had never witnessed such a solemn and touching ceremony.

When the sad news of our great loss reached Cooch Behar a procession was ordered in which officials and relatives walked barefooted to honour the memory of the ruler. The State elephant, of which he had been so fond, accompanied the mourners, and all the while tears rolled down the animal's cheeks, just as if he knew the beloved voice was hushed for ever. The dumb beast's sorrow touched all those who witnessed it, and I always like to think that elephant by some wonderful instinct shared our grief.

We left for India after a fortnight had elapsed, and what can I write about the saddest of all our home-comings? There is nothing more melancholy than the places which our loved ones have deserted and which cry aloud in their desolation.

We had been so happy, I felt that even in Paradise no one could be happier, and I had dreaded the thought of death. But timely or untimely Death had come, and he did not heed the anguish of my heart, he did not hear my cry, nor see my tears; he carried away my dear one and left me behind; my happy days were gone, the future was dark and gloomy, the path of life's journey was thorny and hard. My children were still young, not one of my sons was married, and they clung to me, afraid now that they had lost their father they might lose their mother too. Almost every minute they came into my room to see if I were alive. On my birthday they gave me beautiful flowers, and I sat alone with them, perhaps longer than the children liked, for suddenly Rajey came and called me: "Mother, mother, are you there?"

Life was a blank, the world seemed empty, I felt as if I had no right to be here, as if there was nothing left for me to do. My life, my light, my strength, everything was gone. How could I live without him? Hand in hand we had worked, we had travelled, and now I was left alone with my children. They were loving and dutiful indeed. When I took off my bangles and they saw me in widow's dress they cried: "Mother, will you never wear bracelets again; will you never wear these beautiful ear-rings?" "Yes," I said, "I will when I meet your father in the next world." The boys missed their father more than I can say; he had been more like a brother than a father to them. He had played with them, sung with them, helped them as a friend, and been devoted to them.

Widowhood in India is different from what it is in the West; it is a far harder life. Caste, religion, and custom make it very hard and sad for the widow, whether she be old or young. If a widow laughs loudly or dresses in a way that could possibly be called gay, cruel remarks are made on all sides, and if a Hindu widow gets at all a bad name she suffers greatly at the hands of both her own people and her late husband's. But in spite of all this her undying love for her dead husband brings her closer to the unknown world every hour and every day; through suffering and darkness she knows she is drawing closer to her beloved. My husband made my life like bright sunshine; there were no clouds, no storms, and for the many dear friends I made in the West I shall ever be grateful to him. His trust, his love, his admiration for me were without compare. When I lost him I felt that I had lost all. Women of all nations and all countries envied me once, but now I feel that I shall have to travel alone for the last part of my journey. Once so high I held my head, but now the blow of widowhood has bent it low.

For a few years I felt I ought not to appear before any one or do anything, but my darling children would not have it so.

Chapter XIII

ANOTHER BLOW

A few days after my husband had passed away news of Rajey's succession to the Gadi of Cooch Behar arrived from the Government of India. I was seated on the landing at the Porchester Gate house when my boy came downstairs, knelt by me, clasped his hands on my knee and sobbed. Perhaps he felt his father's loss most at that moment. We had a service in the evening, conducted by my cousin, the Rev. P. L. Sen, at which Rajey's short prayer was most impressive.

He had all his father's effects sealed and brought over to Cooch Behar, and he carried out his father's "will" to the letter.

When Rajey came out to India one of his younger aunts said to him: "You have succeeded your father and you will be like him."

"Like him," was the quick reply, "that is impossible, I can never dare hope to be like my father."

Rajey's attitude towards me in my widowhood was one of absolute devotion. He referred to me in everything, although he treated me like a child and took great care of me. He would not allow any alterations to be made in his father's household, and he always answered when he was taxed with keeping too large a staff, "I cannot dismiss any of them, they were with my father."

His budget was kept unchanged, as he often said he would not live to be thirty-two years of age. I tried all I could to laugh him out of this strange idea, but it was to no purpose. Rajey's belief was founded on his horoscope, which ceased to say anything after thirty-two years. Several fortune-tellers told him the same thing, that he had not a long life written on his hand. I asked a woman palmist to read Rajey's hand and tell me when he would get married. She said: "He has no marriage line on his hand." At Dehra Dun a fortune-teller said the same thing, and an English clairvoyant also foretold his fate at a garden party at Calcutta. I do not think my son allowed his mind to be influenced by these predictions. His melancholy presentiment was due to his ill-health, for I know that he suffered more than he allowed any one to guess.

From the moment of his accession Rajey tried to do his best for Cooch Behar. One of his first acts was to intimate that the Dewan's services were no longer required. "He was never a true friend to my father," was his only comment when the overjoyed natives of Cooch Behar called down blessings on his head for this display of authority.

Rajey also showed the priests that he possessed decided opinions and meant to retain these opinions even in the face of custom and tradition. Before the installation of a Maharajah, it was usual for the priests to perform a Hindu ceremony known as the Abhishek. Rajey declared the Abhishek should not take place. "I do not recognise caste," he said. "But it must be done," declared the State officials. "Who comes next to the priest in my household?" he asked. "Your mother," was the reply. "Then my mother shall act as my priest," he answered. I did the priest's work, for my son would not hear of any one else assisting him.

There was a complete religious ceremony according to the tenets of the New Dispensation at the Installation, and I shall never forget how splendidly Rajey behaved at his Durbar when the Revenue was brought in, and he was acclaimed Maharajah by his subjects. As he sat on his throne, he received symbolic offerings of betel leaf, attar, and flowers. "Take them to my mother," he commanded, and two A.D.C.s brought to me my son's tribute.

At the auspicious hour I was waiting on the balcony with other zenana ladies to see the State procession pass. The elephants were in their gala trappings. The strains of our National Anthem fell on my ears. The troops were in brave array. Suddenly a tall young figure, gorgeous in Raj costume, fell at my feet and paid me homage. It was Rajey! He had actually thought of me in the supreme moment of his life. The grandeur and pageantry were all forgotten. I was the mother whom he delighted to honour, that was the one idea in his mind.

At his second Durbar, while he was dressing, he suddenly looked very grave and said: "This is my last Durbar," and so it proved to be.

I like to recall how my son respected my prejudices. Once, when my husband ruled, I heard that there was a vulgar show at one of the Hindu festivals. I spoke to the Maharajah about it, and he gave orders it should be stopped. Years after Rajey found that the show was again going on, and he was very indignant. I heard that he expressed a wish that "Her Highness's orders should be carried out."

Rajey had no favourites and always sought to do justice. Quiet and dignified, he spoke little and gave few commands, yet all his subjects had the deepest respect for him and tried to avoid his displeasure. Though he was particular about Court pageantry and dress yet his tastes were simple. How thoughtful he was, how loving, how devoted, and yet there was always something sad about him. He seemed more like a prince out of some old legend than a modern young ruler.

Once I was rather annoyed with an Englishman, and remarked to Rajey: "I don't think I can ever forgive him; he is really unpardonable." Rajey looked quite sad, and said: "Oh, mother, I am sure you don't mean it, you don't think it impossible to forgive any one."

I was never relegated to the position of Dowager, but kept up the same state as I had done during his father's lifetime. Rajey was influenced by the advice of Lord Carmichael, who had always been our best friend. "He is a godsend," declared Rajey, and I certainly can never be grateful enough for the help and sympathy which Lord Carmichael always gave to me and mine.

I felt disappointed that Rajey was not given a decoration at the Durbar. Both he and my brother-in-law, the late Maharajah of Mourbhanj, were omitted, which I think was surprising as Rajey was the first ruler in Bengal, and my brother-in-law was the first territorial ruler in Orissa. If it had not been for the latter there would have been no pageant at the show in Calcutta, and it was the pageant which made the show such a success. Their Majesties said it was the best show in Bengal. And Rajey deserved recognition if ever any young ruler did; if the Government had troubled to look into the management of our State they would have found no flaw in its administration. How can young rulers be expected to have any heart to work if their efforts do not meet with encouragement?

Pretty's wedding lightened a little of our sadness at this time. My second girl was engaged to Lionel Mander, a young Englishman who appeared devoted to her. She was just like an English girl, although at home she lived as an Indian Princess. I gave my consent to the marriage, as I had long ago determined to let each of my girls marry the man she loved, and I quite realised that, owing to caste and creed, there would be many difficulties in the way of marriage with any of our princes.

Rajey still seemed very ill and I felt very anxious about him. He seldom complained, but the change in him was painfully apparent. I sometimes begged him to marry, but his answer was always: "No," and once he added: "I have no marriage line on my hand." "What nonsense, darling!" I said. He smiled: "Where shall I put my wife?" "My rooms are quite wasted, Rajey," I answered. He replied: "Mother, your rooms will never be given to another woman while I live. They are always yours, and if ever I marry, I'll build a new palace. Your rooms shall never be taken away."

Rajey went down to Calcutta for a Masonic meeting, but developed ptomaine poisoning and became dreadfully ill. I begged the doctor in attendance to have a consultation, but was told: "Oh, he'll be all right."

I sent for Colonel Browne, but as Rajey had his family doctor (an Englishman) with him, Colonel Browne could say little except that Rajey had better stay in Calcutta as he was too weak to travel. The family doctor, however, insisted on Rajey going to Cooch Behar. Though ill and weak, he started on the trying journey. I was very worried about him, and following him after a couple of days was told that my darling Rajey was anxiously waiting to hear of my arrival. The poor A.D.C. did not know for certain if I had left Calcutta and kept on sending messages to the stations asking if I were coming.

The lives of rulers are in the hands of the doctors appointed by the State. As Rajey was getting more and more ill every day, Jit and Victor in despair besought Colonel Browne to see into things, as they declared their brother's life was in danger. It is strange that the doctors did not think it necessary to have a consultation, but Jit insisted on it, saying: "He is my brother and I shall have doctors from Calcutta." Rajey rallied and was able to entertain Lord and Lady Carmichael at our shoot in April. They thought Rajey seemed in better health and spirits. After our friends had left, Rajey asked what were my plans for the summer. "You are going to England," I said, "let me come with you." That pleased him. I went down to Calcutta a few days before he did. His officers told me that the day he left Cooch Behar the expression on his face was solemn, yet not sad, and that when the National Anthem was played at the station, he stood with clasped hands and eyes bent down. Perhaps he heard the call from above in the music.

Rajey and I, accompanied by his personal staff, arrived in England on the 1st June, 1913. It was a cold morning, and Rajey looked very pale as he entered the special train at Dover, where we were met by my son-in-law, Mr. Ghosal. At the station we found my three girls and a few friends. All thought that Rajey was looking very ill, although they did not say so at the time.

Rajey went to the Curzon Hotel with his staff and I to the Cadogan Hotel, where I stayed with Girlie and Baby for a few weeks. I went to see Rajey almost every day. I was much distressed to find him on the ground floor, and near the telephone, which rang from morning to night. I seldom got news of him. I do not know whom to blame for this, but it made me miserable at the time.

I suppose Rajey was taken to the Derby to brighten him up. It was a cold day and raining. The servants were so careless as to forget to take a great-coat or any wraps, and there he caught a chill and high fever set in. My third brother, who was Rajey's secretary, was anxious to take him away to 3, Palace Court. He was removed there, and the change made him a little better. It was a nice house and Rajey was very pleased with his rooms; but the noise was too trying, as the traffic was constant. To the disappointment of all, Rajey's health did not improve.

Dr. Risien-Russell, who had been called in, begged Rajey to go to a nursing home; he was wonderfully kind to my boy, and Rajey went to a nursing home, where he stayed for a fortnight.

I spoke to him about taking a country house. "My days are numbered," he answered. "I know my time has come. Do you remember, mother dear, how all the fortune-tellers have said I shall not live to be thirty-two?"

Rajey returned to 3, Palace Court from Ascot. This was the beginning of the end. Something in his face forbade me to hope, but I tried to be brave and not let him know how much I suffered. He often had pain which the worn-out frame could hardly endure, and the noise of the traffic prevented much rest when the paroxysms had passed.

He was getting thinner and thinner, and I felt that the case was getting more serious. Still I could not give up hope. One day when he was very ill and could hardly walk, my younger brother helped him to sit down; Rajey put his hand on his head and said: "God bless you, you are a good boy." Another evening when he was very weak, and they feared that he was sinking, he called this brother of mine.

"Bodey, sit down by me; I shall soon be starting on the last long journey."

He sometimes said: "Why does any one fear to die? I am not a bit afraid to go." My Rajey was quite ready for the long journey to the unknown country, where he was going to meet the father he loved so dearly. Once I asked him: "Rajey, don't you wish to live?" He answered: "Mother, I don't wish to die, but if my call has come, if God has sent for me, I shall go, and if I am to go, don't say it is an untimely death. I may be young, but if God sends for me you must believe, mother, that it is a timely death." Another day he said: "I have only one wish, but I don't know whether it will be fulfilled; if only I could die in Cooch Behar."

All sorts of kind messages were sent by our many friends. "Rajey is to live and take care of you," Lady Minto told me.

On the 14th August Rajey was removed to Cromer. It was the end of his sad pilgrimage. As he was lifted out of bed he remarked to his head chauffeur: "Davison, you're taking me away to die." I hid myself in my misery, and as I looked from an upper window I saw Rajey put into the ambulance. I had been asked to go, but I could not as my eyes were too red and I could not hide my feelings. I followed him to Cromer and stayed at the hotel. I used to go to Rajey's house, which was nice and clean and had a pretty little garden. To my eyes Rajey did not look any better, but the doctors thought he was getting on nicely. He had nurses who were good to him, and I shall always be grateful to them.

Just before this Jit had come over from India, as he was going to marry the daughter of the first Hindu Maharajah, the Gaikwar of Baroda. They had been fond of each other for some years, but the

Princess's parents were against the marriage because we were Brahmos and they were Hindus. The Princess came with her parents over to Europe, and Jit followed. It was a most romantic story, as the young couple had seen very little of each other. Yet their love was so strong and true that they promised each other they would marry no one else.

On the 26th August Jit and Indira were married. The ceremonies, civil and religious, took place at the Buckingham Palace Hotel and the Registrar's office. I could not help acknowledging the truth of my father's words that the hand of God is always manifest. In this seemingly impossible union, beset throughout with opposition, I again saw the triumph of the New Dispensation, for my daughter-in-law gave up riches and caste to follow her husband, for love of him. Indira is very clever and very pretty. She knows several languages and has travelled a great deal; for years I had been wanting her to be my daughter-in-law, and I was as fond of her as of my own daughters.

I motored down to Cromer with a friend of mine, Miss Scott, and on our return, the doctor who was attending Rajey gave me hopeful news. He said Rajey was enjoying his food, and in three weeks' time would be out and about. He assured me that we could return to India at the end of October. He even added: "I don't see why His Highness should not play polo again."

On Friday I went to tea with Lady Carmichael's brother, and after dinner I went back again to ask how Rajey was. The doctor said he had a little pain but not much, and he hoped he would be better the next morning. Unfortunately Dr. Russell had to go to London for a few days. Rajey loved him as a friend and had great faith in him.

Very early on Saturday morning a note came from the doctor asking me to go over at once. Over my nightgown I tied on a sari and put over all a thick coat, and in my slippers walked from the hotel to the house with Miss Scott, who was an angel to me that day, and stayed with me in those hours of anguish. I don't remember how, but I managed to get to the door of the house. In the hall, where I met the doctor, I fell. They helped me into the drawing-room and gave me some tea which I could not drink. The doctor asked me if I could be brave and quiet as my son wanted to see me. When Rajey felt the pain, the only thing he had said was: "Nurse, I am in great pain, I want my mother." I kept back my tears and followed the doctor upstairs to the room where Rajey was lying. Never shall I forget my anguish when I looked at him. His lovely eyes were unchanged, but his voice was very faint. "Mother," he whispered, as I bent over him, "I am sinking … I know it."

I too knew it, and oh! how bitter was the knowledge! "Darling, darling," I said, hardly able to speak. He clasped me in his arms, and his face was close to mine. "Raj Rajendra … you know, mother … even the King of kings must die." The long morning passed. I was with him the whole time. Once he said: "I'm leaving you behind, mother." He asked me about Jit and his wife, and also if his youngest uncle were there.

Dr. Risien Russell and my daughter arrived late in the morning. Rajey was pleased to see the doctor, and when he saw my youngest brother he caught hold of his hand tight as if it were the last grip of his friendship. I felt that if Dr. Russell had not been there, I should have had no friend in my great trouble. He was a godsend to me.

On Sunday, at midnight, surrounded by those who were near and dear to him, Rajey breathed his last. Thirty-one years ago this boy had brought me every possible happiness. Now the world is dark and gloomy, and I do not know how I shall travel the last part of my journey, so heavy-laden am I with my grief. Rajey was not an ordinary son to me. His birth had made every difference in my life. The Cooch Beharis would never have been so friendly towards me had it not been for my Rajey's coming; neither could I have had so happy a home had Rajey not arrived. God gave him to me and God has taken him away. He was the most precious gift I had; but I know, I believe that I shall meet him again in the Land of Everlasting Happiness. These pangs of my heart will cease when I am called to be with my two precious ones.

Rajey was dressed in his chupkan and a sacred coloured shawl was thrown over him. Wreaths of flowers were sent by kind friends, and his room looked no longer like a mourning room but like a paradise.

My Rajey had put on the garment of immortality. His painful journey was ended, and in the heaven whither his spirit had flown, he had already been welcomed by his father, and together they await me there.

But what remained for me? I had to suffer the long days and the misery of the hours when sleep forsook me and grief kept a watch by my pillow. I had to live and think that to live is sometimes the worst torture that can be inflicted on mankind. How often have I proved to myself the truth of those lines:

"'Tis hard to smile when one would weep,

To speak when one would silent be:

To wake when one would wish to sleep,

185

And wake in agony."

Now was repeated the sad ceremonial of two years ago, when my husband's body was committed to the flames. Only two years and the Ideal Ruler and the Child of Promise had both vanished from our eyes. Surely we shall never understand the workings of Divine Providence. All that our sad souls can do is to trust in the infinite wisdom of God.

The blank his loss has left in my life will always be there, but he must have gone to do a greater work, and the thought of this is the only thing that gives me comfort.

Countless were the telegrams and letters of sympathy I received, and the kindness of all my friends touched me very much. The late Duchess of Connaught sent word from Bagshot: "We all deeply sympathise with you in your great loss. We look back with pleasure to the time when Rajey used to stay with us."

We sent the ashes of our beloved back to Cooch Behar, and they rest beside those of his father in the marble mausoleum which has been built in the rose garden. This old garden is a peaceful spot. Long ago the Maharajah learned his lessons in the ruined summer-house which still stands on the borders of the lake, where in bygone times the Maharanis used to bathe, and many legends are connected with the place. The scented stillness is now unbroken save for the music of the birds, and the mournful whisperings of the trees when the wind speaks to them of the sleepers.

This rose garden is walled in on three sides, and from it can be seen the snow hills far away. There are masses of roses and lilies, and it is impossible to describe the fragrance of the flowers. Rajey and his father are surrounded by Peace. Prayers are offered there every evening, and sometimes the boys go there alone in the moonlight.

My love is so strong that I think Death has opened the door of Eternity a little way for me, and my dear ones are nearer to me than ever. Long ago I saw the roses of youth blooming at Belghuria. Later, the crimson flowers of love were mine, but the sweetest of all flowers to me are those of remembrance, which shed their petals year after year over the ashes of my dear ones who wait for me on the radiant shore.

"Take them, O Grave! and let them be

Folded upon thy narrow shelves,

As garments of the soul laid by,

And precious only to ourselves.

"Take them, O great Eternity!

Our little life is but a gust

That bends the branches of thy tree

And trails its blossoms in the dust."

Chapter XIV

VICEROYS I HAVE KNOWN

Lord Lytton knew me as a little girl in India, but we did not meet again until 1887 when I was visiting England. I went with my husband to the Foreign Office party one evening. It was a grand affair and I had a very nice dress. We were all standing in a line waiting for the Royal procession to pass when Lord Lytton saw me. He came and stood by me and putting his arm round my waist said: "You have grown, and look so pretty, but so grown-up." I felt very uncomfortable and kept on saying: "Oh, Lord Lytton, but I am so old. Do you know I am the mother of three children? Do please remember that I am an old woman, over twenty." In his kind voice he said: "It was only the other day I saw you at your father's school, a little, little girl."

Lord and Lady Ripon were very kind to us. In his time the Ilbert Bill was passed, which made a great sensation in India and the English spoke against the Indians and Lord Ripon. One English lady said to me: "Why was such a man as Lord Ripon sent out to India? he goes against his Queen." I am sure the lady did not know what she was saying, as Lord Ripon was a friend to India and thus served Her Majesty the late Queen well. When my darling little Rajey had typhoid fever in Simla in 1882 both Lord and Lady Ripon constantly made kind inquiries and offered their doctor Anderson, a clever and charming man.

Lord Dufferin is supposed to have been the cleverest Viceroy in India; I was so ignorant about politics I cannot say much about his administrative work, but I do know that he was a very kind personal friend of mine. Lady Dufferin was the most clever and capable Vicereine that has ever been out in India. She once came to one of my "sari" dinners, when we all wore saris, sat on the floor, and ate with our fingers. One of the A.D.C.s remarked that Her Excellency looked like a goddess.

Lady Dufferin wrote a book on India in which she said a great deal about my dear mother, whom she greatly admired. I think she was amazed to see how cheerfully mother gave up all the comforts of life after she lost my father. Lady Dufferin showed the greatest interest in all my father's institutions, and we were very proud when Lord Dufferin presented a medal to the Victoria College. Lady Dufferin founded the Delhi Hospital, where Indian women are trained to be doctors and midwives. When Lady Dufferin asked me about it and if it would be a success, I said, "Yes," but did not quite understand about it or realise the difficulties. It is difficult to make my Western sisters understand about caste prejudice in my country. When Lady Dufferin first began this training much discussion went on all over India. To begin with, women of high caste could not do work of the kind as they thought it lowered their position; secondly, zenana ladies, however poor, did not wish to be trained or study with men, therefore in the beginning only very common women took up the medical profession, but now many advanced women have taken it up and have studied hard and taken degrees, thus serving their country, for which we owe much gratitude to Lady Dufferin. Lady Wenlock told me not long ago that the idea was originally Lady Ripon's, but she was unable to carry it out before she left India.

Lord and Lady Lansdowne were the greatest Viceroy friends we ever had. We all, the whole family, loved and admired them and their children. The Maharajah was treated as a personal friend of theirs, which made the other Maharajahs very jealous. When I was very ill once, Lady Lansdowne used to come and see me, and they were most kind to Rajey. Once H.H. the Begum of Bhopal gave a strict purdah party and I was invited to meet Lady Lansdowne. I do not quite remember, but I think the Resident wanted to know who should sit in the next highest seat to Lady Lansdowne, and he was informed that I was to sit next to the Viceroy's wife, which the Resident did not like at all. When I heard of this I thought I would not go, but kind Lady Lansdowne on being informed of it sent I do not know what message to the Begum's official. Anyway the whole tone of the letters changed, I was begged to go, and on my arrival at the party I found that H.H. the Begum had placed Lady Lansdowne in a chair on her right hand and I was to sit in a chair on her left hand; these were the only seats, all the other guests came and shook hands with the Begum while we were seated.

Lady Lansdowne was kindness itself to my children. She never made any distinction between English and Indians at her parties, and her tactful consideration made her very popular. I think her charming mind was reflected in her beautiful face.

I was at my happiest in Lord Lansdowne's reign; everything seemed to be so bright in my life at that time, and I often think now of that happy past. Lord Lansdowne once said: "My house is not half large enough to hold all the people you and the Maharajah entertain in camp." I did appreciate those kind words.

Lord Elgin was a kind Viceroy; I don't know whether he did much as a statesman, but he was a very kind easy-going man. Lady Elgin gave some very cheery children's parties. At one of these my Jit kept on having so much ice cream that I am sure all the A.D.C.s and servants must have longed for us to leave the table. I went to Calcutta once for a few hours, the Viceroy heard of it and asked me if I would dine with them quietly; it was no party, only a family gathering. This was a great honour. I did not think I could have a maid with me, so I sent for a hair-dresser. He was told not to be long, but perhaps he felt artistic that evening, for he went on making curls and waves and using hundreds of hairpins. I was most impatient and kept reminding him of the time, but it had no effect. The consequence was that I was about half an hour late, a thing I shall never forget. When I arrived, I found the two A.D.C.s in despair, sitting on the steps watching the gate. One of them was the late Captain Adams. I did not know how to make my excuses and had to tell the unpleasant truth, that it was the fault of the hair-dresser, but all they did was to pay nice compliments. I was so nervous when I went up into the drawing-room that I felt like running away, but when Lord and Lady Elgin came in and I made my apologies, Lord Elgin said: "Please don't be sorry; I am grateful to you for being a little late. You know it is the English mail day, and you gave me a little extra time to write a few more letters, for which I have to thank you." This made me forget all my troubles and only remember what a proud and happy woman I was.

There was much splendour in the time of the Curzons, but I don't believe that Lord Curzon was ever really in sympathy with us. He is a very clever man; but, may I be forgiven for my frankness, I found him slightly interfering in private matters. He was too unapproachable, which was most regrettable. I consider that he missed many golden opportunities. Lady Curzon was handsome and charming, but to my great disappointment I had neither the pleasure nor the honour of knowing her well.

Lord Curzon did a lot of good to the country; and tried to revive the old industries, the saris, cashmeres, etc. Also he put up tablets on great men's birth places and homes, which was much appreciated; but he interfered with the future of the Indian Princes' young sons. Whether the fathers were willing or not he did not wait to find out, but forced them to send their boys into the Cadet Corps, and by so doing many boys lost their opportunities of learning administrative work. Of course, we had to submit because no one wishes to be in the Viceroy's bad books.

Lord and Lady Minto we admired and liked very much. Lord Minto was so kind a friend that although he was Viceroy he helped a zemindar at the cost of much trouble to himself. Lady Minto was the first to ask the purdah ladies to Government House. She gave parties for them regularly every year while she was in Calcutta and the ladies enjoyed them enormously. I remember a Hindu lady remarking of Lady Minto: "I do like her smile so." My sister and the Maharani of Burdwan and I joined together and gave three parties to Lady Minto at Woodlands, and I got up some tableaux which both the English and Indian ladies enjoyed. On one occasion I dressed Lady Minto in a Bengali bridal dress, scarlet and gold, and she looked lovely. Lady Minto told me afterwards that when she returned to Government House she sent a message to the military secretary that a Maharani was waiting in the hall, and when he came and found Lady Minto in the bridal dress for a moment he thought it really was a Maharani.

I remember a Bengali gentleman of high position telling us once: "Lord Minto is a thorough gentleman; when I and my friend went to call on him he was so nice and made us feel quite at home. What struck us most was that at the close of the visit, when we were going away, Lord Minto, instead of calling an orderly or an A.D.C., walked up to the door and opened it himself. We felt uncomfortable, but it was a gentlemanly action; by opening the door he lost nothing, and we gained so much."

I feel it my duty to allude to something that happened in Lord Minto's reign. A rumour was circulated that a most loyal British subject was disloyal to the Government. I was horrified when I heard the lie; it reached the highest circles. Even Sir O'Moore Creagh, then Commander-in-Chief, may have credited it. Perhaps it was some fellow-countryman who started this unpardonable lie; but how could the Government believe such an impossible thing? I only hope that whoever did this great wrong will confess his wickedness before he leaves this world.

Lord Hardinge did a lot of good to many people, but he was never very kindly disposed to the Cooch Behar Raj family. Soon after I lost my husband we came back to India, and as I had received nothing but kindness from the Royal Family and from so many Viceroys, I expected that Lord Hardinge as Viceroy would be kind to me. But on the contrary he did not seem to take any trouble to be kind to my son. When our present King was at the Delhi Durbar Lord Hardinge paid many visits to the other Maharajahs, but never thought of leaving his card on the Maharajah of Cooch Behar, which was not only an insult to the Maharajah but to the whole of Bengal. Lord Hardinge also interfered with our private affairs, at which I was surprised because we liked him and thought him clever and never opposed him.

Here I might mention that at this Delhi Durbar a certain Political Officer visited the Maharajah's camp in ordinary lounge clothes, a thing which even H.M. the King would not think of doing. Such Englishmen should have attention drawn to them and their manners corrected.

Lord Carmichael, when Governor of Bengal, was a most kind friend to my Rajey and to me. Words are too poor to express my gratitude to him.

Some years ago a branch of the London National Indian Association was opened in Calcutta, where Western and Eastern ladies met. For a few years the Association did wonderful work. Many strict purdah ladies came to it, and many of us gave parties. Lady Jenkins gave a fancy-dress ball and all the purdah ladies were in fancy costume; it was a brilliant sight. Lady Holmwood took great trouble for the Association, and we all hoped soon to have a permanent building for it. Then one of the members spoke against others and the whole thing nearly fell through. But Lady Carmichael with her kind heart and tact managed to gather the ladies together again and make them work hand in hand for our soldiers during the war. Very few, I fear, take interest in the Association now.

Lord Ronaldshay, the present Governor, we like very much; he is very popular in Bengal and a brilliant speaker. He is clever, and has studied India well, and I do not think there are many subjects on which he cannot talk; it is a treat to get a chance of speaking to him on serious subjects. I did not know Lady Ronaldshay until she came out to Jit's shooting camp in Cooch Behar. She is a sweet and good mother and just like an ordinary lady when surrounded by her children.

Of all the wives of the Lieutenant-Governors in Bengal Lady (Charles) Elliott was the cleverest. Sir William Duke was a kind personal friend to us all.

I have not known many Americans, but among the few I have met some were very nice; a Mrs. Perrier was charming. I know one American lady, when she was out in India, spoke very angrily to an Englishman whom she found treating an Indian gentleman as if he were a porter or a servant. Yet another American woman once refused to sit in the stalls of a London theatre because an Indian lady was seated close to her. Some Canadians are like the latter, and I hope they will never come to India, to disgrace their country and sex. Such women could never belong to or understand universal sisterhood.

I never had the pleasure of knowing any Australians until a few months ago when I returned from England by P. and O. Mantua. There were some charming Australians on board. The ladies were smart and clever, with delightful manners. It really was a great pleasure to me to meet them. One lady in particular I found most pleasant.

I had the pleasure of knowing Lord Kitchener well. One could hardly believe that such a fine big soldier could be such a charming host; his parties were always successful. When the Prince of Wales (now our King) was out in Calcutta we were talking about Lord Kitchener, and H.R.H. said to me that he had given a perfect dinner-party. I answered that perhaps it would have been more perfect if he had had a Lady Kitchener there. But the Prince said: "There I do not agree with you. Lord Kitchener is a perfect host even without a Lady Kitchener."

I hope I shall be forgiven if my readers do not find much about politics in this book, but I have never been interested in politics, and I think it is better for women not to take part in political work. It is another thing though for the mothers and wives of rulers in India to complain of the Government if they find it interfering with them. There are mothers and wives of rulers in Bengal and the Punjab who know very little or no English and cannot approach the Government direct but have to be represented by the Anglo-Indian Commissioners or Political Agents. And I regret to say that the Government officials now are often of a different type from those in olden days, and this causes trouble in the country. Some of these Englishmen do not know how to talk or to write to Indian ladies, neither do they know how to address gentlemen. Most of these civilians are sent out simply because they have passed the Civil Service Examination; how can any polite manners be expected of them? Yet whoever visits England once wishes to go there again, and the chief reason of this is, that the English are much nicer to Indians in England than they are in India. I always say that as long as the Government respect and consider Indian women the throne is safe; history itself shows that when women are ill-treated no rule is secure.

Once I wished to see Lord Curzon, and had he seen me some very great unpleasantness might have been avoided. I fully expected to get a letter written by his own hand, instead of that Mr. , the secretary, replied to this effect: "H.E. wishes the Maharajah to write him if there is anything wanted." If Lord Curzon only heard and knew how Mr. H, our Superintendent, treated matters in connection with my private life and things I hold sacred I am sure he would not have hesitated to see me. Some of these officials seem to enjoy calling us untruthful. Well, Mr. H should feel happy to know that his official "confidential box," which he left in the care of the late Calica Das, containing papers against the Maharajah's family, has been found and is now public property. Mr. L. was once our Superintendent; he gave the idea to Government that the Cooch Behar Raj family was most extravagant, and unfortunately the members of the family never had the chance to inform the Government what the Superintendents themselves spent. I asked Mr. L. to have a little bamboo shed built at Woodlands, which would have cost perhaps about £2; the Maharajah was away in England at the time. Mr. L. said he must get the sanction of His Highness; the cablegram would probably have cost him £2; and if I remember rightly in the same year Mr. L. expended £8000 on a house in Darjeeling which, though not sanctioned, H.H. had to pay; such can be the power and folly of a Superintendent.

When Victor was doing well at Eton and becoming quite a grand cricketer to the great satisfaction of the Maharajah, Lord Curzon was appointed Viceroy, and we were all anxious to know what to do and how to please him. It was known he did not like Indian boys being educated in England, and as a Maharajah himself cannot always approach a Viceroy about family affairs, and I happened to know one of the high officials well, I asked him for advice. By his advice I had dear Victor brought back to India and thus all his future career was spoilt as he was sent to the Cadet Corps. This Corps ruined the future of many young lives; it was a waste of money and time. After it had failed the Maharajah sent Vic to Cuba for agricultural training, to learn something about tobacco, which grows all over Cooch Behar. When Vic returned home after a few years the Maharajah had machines brought out from America and a nice piece of land prepared for the tobacco, but because of Mr. H, who was then Superintendent, the whole thing fell through.

Our religion of the New Dispensation teaches loyalty to the Throne. This loyal feeling is a sacred duty to me, and in the whole of India no family is more loyal to His Gracious Majesty than the Cooch Behar Raj family.

Chapter XV

LATER YEARS

My dear Jit has begun his work well and is doing his best to make the State prosperous. His love for his people is deep and he takes great interest in administration. He works hard and sometimes sits at his table and writes till midnight. He looks into every detail himself, and I often wonder how he can do so much: a boy who was never brought up as the heir. How I long for my dear husband to come and see his Jit working for the good of the State. He built a hospital in Lord Carmichael's name, and has done many things to improve the health of the people, but unfortunately during his reign we have had the dreadful Western War from which the country has suffered much. Such things as rice and potatoes have been sent out of the State, and jute could not be exported. Everything has been very high in price, more than double. Jit has increased the salaries of the officers, and the pay of the servants, besides giving numberless subscriptions and donations, and helping in the War Loan; but he does things quietly and no one knows of them. He has five children, three girls and two boys; they are all lovely, especially the eldest girl. Jit is a clever man and has written some charming poems and books. It is hard for him that all the old officers now are either dead or retired and he has to work with new and untried men, but he takes it quite coolly.

One day he said to me: "Mother, if we believe that God is all-merciful, we shall never ask Him 'Why?' We may think father has gone too soon. He was young and strong and many lives depended on him, but God is merciful and God knows best. If God loves us he would not do anything that would hurt us. It is all for the best, and we must believe it." Jit has been one of the best of sons to me, so loving, so kind and thoughtful, and he often treats me as if I were the same age as his little daughter.

Victor is a wonderful brother. I do not think in the wide world any one could find a more unselfish and affectionate brother than he is to Jit. Anything that Jit says is law to him. He would give his life for his brother; he would go to the ends of the earth to get anything that would make his brother happy. In his life Jit comes first. Victor has married the daughter of a distant cousin of mine, a pretty girl. They have two children, both boys. Victor's wife is called Nirupoma; she is of the same faith as we are, a Brahmo. She is well educated and edits a magazine in Bengali. She is devoted to her husband and children.

Baby has married Alan Mander, the younger brother of Lionel. I did not wish her to marry so young nor to part with her so soon, especially as it was only six months after I had lost my Rajey, but now my life has come to that stage that I must not be heard, my love must pray silently for the happiness of my children. They are very precious and their happiness is my happiness. Baby wished to marry this boy; he is fine-looking, and has travelled a good deal, and as he was anxious to have the wedding soon I did not stand in the way, and they were married at Woodlands on the 25th February, 1914. During the War he was in the Army and now they are in England. Alan has been a very good son-in-law; I don't think I could have had a better, even in fancy.

Among the Maharajahs of India I know but few. The Maharajahs of Bikanir and Gwalior call me "Mother;" the former was at school at Mayo College with Rajey. The Maharajah of Kapurthala was like a brother to my husband; the Maharajah of Idar I know very well. In India there are very few Maharanis, perhaps none except myself, who come out, so it is difficult to get to know them, and without a special invitation one cannot visit their States. Some of the Maharajahs could do much for their country. Surely there is enough money in India to revive its ancient history and search out its ruined palaces and temples; but the Maharajahs seldom meet together to discuss these things, and that is perhaps why our Western visitors do not know much of our ancient India.

During the last few years I have travelled a little, and would like to tell my readers something about my country. Once I went on a Hindu pilgrimage to a place called Hardwar. In my book "Nine Ideal Indian Women," there is a story about Sati; near Hardwar is Sati's birthplace, an old palace now in ruins, and this I and my third sister went to see. Among the ruins are said to be dozens of cobras, but they do not hurt any one. We sat on the steps that led down to the river and had a little service. There was a feeling about the whole place, even after these thousands of years, as if it had been the home of a beautiful soul and was near the spiritual world. We gazed upon the beautiful scene: the wonderful old ruined palace with its flights of steps leading down to the deep blue river, and in the distance the pure white snows of the Himalayas. We noticed a strange thing as we sat there; in the middle of the river was a tiny island, and on this a tortoise was playing with a snake; one would never have thought that a snake and a tortoise could be together, yet here they were like two friends.

In that same book of mine is the story of Harischandra and the burning ghat; that ghat still remains in Benares. We sisters went there to see it one day after sunset in a boat kindly lent to us by the Maharajah of Benares. Down the stream floated hundreds of little lights; it looked as if the Ganges had rows of necklaces round her throat. It was an impressive sight; on the banks and down in the water were thousands of men and women with clasped hands and down-bent heads, saying their evening prayers near the ghat where the Maharajah Harischandra worked disguised as a chandal.

Nearly two years ago I came from Simla to meet my sister, who was waiting for me to go with her on a pilgrimage to Sarag-duar (the Door of Heaven). We planned to go by train to a station near the place, and as there was no passenger train about that time a railway carriage had to be attached to a goods train. When we arrived at the station some of our party went in tongas and for my sister and me a friend sent a carriage, the best that could be had, but very ordinary in our eyes. We started off happily. It was a very rough rocky road, but our hearts were full of the Sarag-duar and we were longing for the end of the journey. My sister's two little children who were with us behaved wonderfully, and did not complain of either hunger or fatigue. After several hours we arrived at the river-side. It was early in the morning, the sky was bright blue, at our feet the Ganges flowed between high banks, and tall trees guarded the Door of Heaven. Two boats were waiting and we crossed the river. As we went over I felt as if I must say to the river: "May you take me on my last crossing even as you take me to the Door of Heaven to-day."

We arrived at the Sarag-duar; it was still beautifully cool and fresh, and as my sister had brought fruit and sweets we sat there and refreshed ourselves. While we were eating, a message arrived from one of the holy men that he would like to see us, and after a few minutes he came. What a good and handsome face he had! He was dressed in an almond-coloured (sacred) robe and brought fruit and flowers for us. His good words dropped on our hearts like cool water on an aching brow. When he saw my sister's children he said he must send some milk for them, and soon after he had left us warm milk came. In this little land of peace there is one house in which food is cooked once a day for the hermits and the pilgrims, of whom there are thousands in the summer months and hundreds in the cold weather. In the fields are splendid cows. Gifts of money are made by some generous friends and this pays for the food. It is a wonderful place, so peaceful, so beautiful; whoever visits it, whatever his religion, must feel that it is indeed near heaven. Far away are blue hills, and nearer great plains over which herds of wild elephant, tigers, and leopards roam, but do no harm. Some of the hermits live among the roots of the big trees, and even in the winter months when the cold is very severe they bathe daily in the river. No women are allowed in that holy place, nor any families; we were allowed to halt there a few hours as a special favour because we were my father's daughters. There is no smoke of cooking, no shouting, no cry of children; all is peace; even the river is calm and quiet.

From there we went to the place where Harischandra's brother Lachman spent his last days, and had to cross the river by a bridge of planks which shakes all the time one walks. As we went we saw jutting out into the stream the piece of rock on which Dhruba, when a little boy, knelt one day to pray to his God and was much disturbed by the loud noise of the waters. So Dhruba addressed the river and said: "Mother Ganges, how can my prayers reach the feet of God if you disturb me so; how can my mind be quiet while such loud sounds go on?" And it is a curious thing that just where Dhruba sat the river is perfectly calm, while a few yards off on the other side of the rock the water boils and rushes. We bathed in the river; it was icy cold but it gave us new strength and new hope.

I should so much like my Western sisters to see some of these peaceful holy spots. Unfortunately there is no history of India in which all the old stories are told; they would make the country so much more interesting to the traveller. India is not the country some Western writers make it out to be. It is an ancient land and a spiritual. Modern ideas, to my thinking, often make young people hard and perhaps selfish. If we do not love each other can we do good to any one? In the old history of India unselfish love was given to one and all, and the crown of India was love. We are lucky indeed to be the children of such a country, but are we worthy of that love, have we forgotten what our ancestors did? Learn all the good you can from other countries, but remain an Indian still is my poor advice. Hurting others cannot make us Indians happy. I am so proud of being an Indian. Let the world know how beautiful and good India's daughters were, and let us try and follow in their footsteps; in their time Love and Peace reigned. Love will bring us all together and make India once more happy and rich. A number of Western authors make great mischief by writing things that are not true. One lady, Maud Diver, I know has written many untrue things about us, and I am afraid people who do not know us will believe the worst. It is a great mistake to write such things; one by one we shall all go, but our letters and books will remain for the next generation to read.

I often feel that if Her Majesty would include a Maharani among her ladies, she would get to know the Indians much better; she is so fond of anything Indian and takes so much interest in India that it would help her, especially at such a time as this. Her Majesty might take a lady from each Presidency in turn, changing her every four months; and if His Majesty also would choose an Indian of noble birth from each Presidency, changing him in the same way every four months, I am sure it would keep Their Majesties informed of the state of feeling throughout the whole of India, and they would gain first-hand and correct information. Much mischief is often done because things have to go through so many channels. I might mention here that sometimes the representatives of His Majesty are not very sympathetic nor tactful with the Indians. Indians do not get asked to parties as they used to be, and it is only natural they should expect to be invited by the high officials in India who represent their Emperor.

The last time I visited England was in order to be with Baby for the first arrival in her family. I got there on the 13th June, 1920, and went to Baby's house, where I was very comfortable. Her little girl was born on the 8th July at 7, Lyall Street, a house which Baby had rented. The dear newborn delighted our hearts. We thanked God for her safe arrival. It is our custom to have a children's feast on the eighth day after the birth. On the following week we had all the children from the garage next door and some others to tea. Each of them and every member of the household staff received a little souvenir of our happiness.

When Baby was strong enough to be moved she returned to her house at Kingston and I visited her there. Suddhira and Alan gave up their room to me and occupied the drawing-room, which was not at all comfortable for them, still we were all very happy at being together.

In September I moved up to town to Grosvenor Street, where I had rented a house from a rich lady. Our stay there would have been a happier one had it not been for the continual annoyance of receiving unpleasant messages from the owner. Oh, what a worry the house problem in England is nowadays!

Since I lost my dear husband I had lived in a very retired way. Now in Grosvenor Street I began to see a few old friends, and this happy intercourse recalled to me the golden days of my life. I had the great pleasure of meeting Lord and Lady Lansdowne, General Birdwood, Colonel and Mrs. Burn, Lord and Lady Suffield, General and Lady Blood, the latter as cheery as ever. Lady Hewitt, Mrs. Roberts, Mrs. Beverley and others. Lady Headfort was as kind as ever. I had the great honour of going to see Their Majesties and stayed to tea with them. I went to see Her Majesty Queen Alexandra. How sad it made me to see her so changed! This was the first time Her Majesty spoke sadly. H.R.H. Princess Beatrice was the same gracious and kind Princess. I had the honour of having tea with her. Miss Minnie Cochrane, a lady-in-waiting to the Princess, is a very dear friend of mine and it made me so happy to meet her again. I also went to see H.R.H. the Duke of Connaught. How it saddened me when I met him all alone in his drawing-room! In the days of the past, H.R.H. the Duchess and her children filled the house with their merriment. My heart went out to the Duke in his loneliness. I compared myself with this Royal Prince. He had lost his life's companion and his first-born, and my husband and eldest son are both gone. H.R.H. was most kind and sympathetic.

Just as I was beginning to revive old friendships and go about a little there came the crushing sad news of my poor darling Hitty's last illness. How shall I bear his loss! I am no longer young and sorrows have worn away my strength. I am nearing the end of life's journey, oh, why have I suffered this terrible blow? Why was my Hitty called away so early? His life was hardly begun and it is ended! The half-opened flower of his manhood is for ever closed. Before I left for England I had put aside jewels and household silver-ware for him, hoping he would marry soon. I was prepared to go, I thought that perhaps my ashes would be brought back from England, but he is gone and I still linger here. How cruel it seemed to me; what great sorrow I suffered! Only a mother who has lost her boy can realise the anguish. If we could but have a glimpse of our happy departed dear ones in the realms of bliss what consolation it would be to our bereaved aching hearts!

Jit was sweet in those dark days. How he tried to comfort me. He said: "Mother, be brave, be brave. Trust in God, mother—God does everything for the best. Hitty is happier there than he was here. He is with father and Dada." Jit said many kind and comforting words; how I love him for his gentleness! Indira, too, was very kind and often came and spoke consolingly. Suddhira and Alan were a help and comfort to me. I do not know what I should have done at that time had they not come and stayed with me. Suddhira often cooked for me, and she looked after and nursed me as if she were the mother and I her child. Her loving devotion touched me deeply. What a sweet true daughter she proved herself in those days of bitter bereavement! Her little baby girl was a real blessing, and seemed a bright messenger from above bringing hope from our heavenly home.

In February I left England and arrived in Bombay on the 26th of the same month. Jit and Indira were there on their way to Calcutta. I arrived at Howrah on the 1st March, the anniversary of the day when our mother was taken from us. Victor met me, and with him were my brother and other relations. How I missed my Hitty. I went straight to Lily Cottage, where we had a short "In memoriam" service. Monica was there, and after the service I went to my sister Sucharu's, where Bino and others were waiting. One and all wept over my sad loss. They were all devoted to dear Hitty, and Victor in particular feels the parting.

Dear Hitty is resting now near his father and brother in the palace garden, where all is quiet and still, and the scent of the flowers seems to speak of the sweetness of heaven. His voice is hushed and no one will ever again look upon his dear face, but his soul lives on in the Land Immortal where he has been called to greater work. I am longing to be with my loved ones who have gone before, to be where we shall never part again.

This sad loss has brought a great change into my life. I feel the unknown world is very near to me and I must try and finish what I think I have to do quickly. God gifted me with everything that was precious, and one thing I wish to leave behind me and that is Love. I feel my strength has gone and often wonder why I am left. I had a house with four walls like rock and a strong roof that sheltered me, and now the roof is gone and two of the walls are down. The happy past is very far away, and I seem to be living in a different world. Life goes on, days and months have passed laden with sorrow and grief, but I am still walking on the edge of this life. My only wish now is to serve my family and my people and my Church, the Church of the New Dispensation.

It is my happiness to know that Jit and Victor are working hand in hand for the welfare of Cooch Behar. Jit's great ambition is to make his State a model one, and he is always eager to help forward its progress.

Some of the Governors of Bengal have been most kind to my school at Darjeeling, where sixty or seventy children of all castes are taught kindergarten, and I am glad to say it does very well indeed. My technical school for poor Hindu ladies in Calcutta too is a success. The Victoria College was established by my dear father for the better education of women.

We often used to speak of a terrible tragedy which happened in our own family through a relation not knowing how to read.

This lady's son was ill with typhoid, but he got better rapidly and one day the doctor told the mother the patient might eat a little solid food. After the doctor had left, two bottles of medicine arrived. The happy mother at once insisted that the boy should take a dose to hasten his recovery. But, alas! one of the bottles contained liniment for external use only, and this happened to be the bottle picked up by her. The boy died in great agony. The poor mother became almost insane with grief when she found out that she was the unwitting cause of her son's end. This is one of the many stories of what has happened in Hindu homes where the ladies are kept from the knowledge of reading and writing. It is no wonder therefore that we have tried hard for education for our country-women. But we found it uphill work for many years.

My father founded other institutions, but they do not all exist now because of lack of finances, but we do not despair, where there is a will there is a way and Indian women are not so ignorant as Western people think. In the zenanas you will find fine characters, educated up-to-date women, good nurses, clever accountants, sweet singers, most loving mothers, and devoted wives, and as far as looks go, it is hard to beat a real Indian beauty. I have an ambition, if I live, to have an Asram for gentlefolk where they can live in peace and receive instruction, and it is my great hope that before many years have passed Indian women will stand in their right place and once again India will cry aloud: "I am proud of my daughters."

THE END